LONGBURROW

THE BEASTS OF GRIMHEART

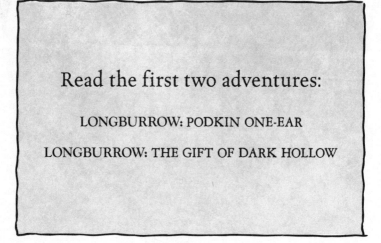

Read the first two adventures:

LONGBURROW: PODKIN ONE-EAR

LONGBURROW: THE GIFT OF DARK HOLLOW

LONGBURROW

THE BEASTS OF
GRIMHEART

KIERAN LARWOOD

ILLUSTRATIONS BY DAVID WYATT

CLARION BOOKS
HOUGHTON MIFFLIN HARCOURT
BOSTON   NEW YORK

Clarion Books

3 Park Avenue

New York, New York 10016

Copyright © 2018 by Kieran Larwood
Illustrations copyright © 2018 by David Wyatt

First U.S. edition, 2019
First published in the U.K. in 2018 by Faber and Faber Limited

Clarion Books is an imprint of Houghton Mifflin Harcourt Publishing Company.

hmhbooks.com

The text was set in Celestia Antiqua Std.
Designed by Lisa Vega

Library of Congress Cataloging-in-Publication Data
Names: Larwood, Kieran, author. | Wyatt, David, 1968–illustrator.
Title: The beasts of Grimheart / Kieran Larwood ; illustrations by David Wyatt.
Description: First U.S. edition. | Boston ; New York : Clarion Books,
Houghton Mifflin Harcourt, 2019. | Series: Longburrow ; [2] | "First
published in 2018 by Faber and Faber Limited." | Summary: "The
young rabbit Podkin One-Ear and his allies battle to save their
land from the evil Gorm tribe"— Provided by publisher.
Identifiers: LCCN 2018051122 (print) | LCCN 2018055198 (ebook) |
ISBN 9781328632548 (ebook) | ISBN 9781328696021 (hardback)
Subjects: | CYAC: Rabbits— Fiction. | Brothers and sisters— Fiction. | Adventure
and adventurers— Fiction. | Fantasy. | BISAC: JUVENILE FICTION / Action &
Adventure / General. | JUVENILE FICTION / Animals / Rabbits. | JUVENILE
FICTION / Fantasy & Magic. | JUVENILE FICTION / Family / Siblings.
Classification: LCC PZ7.L3263 (ebook) |
LCC PZ7.L3263 Be 2019 (print) | DDC [Fic]—dc23
LC record available at https://lccn.loc.gov/2018051122

Manufactured in the United States of America
DOC 10 9 8 7 6 5 4 3 2 1
4500762656

To Piper

CONTENTS

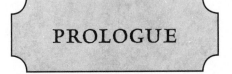

PROLOGUE

Back in the first days, it is said, the goddesses Estra and Nixha came to Lanica and banished Gormalech the World Eater underground. Then they set about filling the place with life (and death, because that was Nixha's job): plants, trees, insects, fish, and, of course, rabbits.

They chose rabbits to run the world, walking and talking as the Ancients before them once had. They gave them fire and shelter, even twelve magic Gifts to keep them safe.

But something was missing.

Estra realized that living — *properly* living — is nothing without the power to *think* about it. To think, talk, and sing and to pass on those thoughts and ideas to those who come after you (once Nixha has done her work) so that they can use them, build on them, and add to them.

Life, the Goddess thought, *is one big story.* And she needed someone to tell it.

So she called upon Clarion to join them, and he became the god of songs and tales. He chose certain rabbits to be his bards, and he gave them this blessing: the ability to tap into the realm of ideas and creation whenever they wanted, to look at the world in a slightly different way and then pass it on through a word, a tune, or an image.

And so the Five Realms were filled with songs, stories, plays, poems, and paintings, and it was a much better place for it.

Such a thing, the bards decided, needed a celebration (and bards *really* like celebrating), so they chose to gather every year at a valley in the Razorback Downs, where Enderby meets Orestad, and the ring of obsidian stones known as Blackhenge sparkles in the spring sunshine.

There they could drink, dance, get their ears tattooed, and, most importantly, share and spread their stories and songs with other bards from all over the Five Realms of Lanica.

The celebration was known as the Festival of Clarion: a tent city full of noise and color, complete with a contest to find the High Bard's champion. An organized riot of singing, performing, and mead drinking, where old friends reunited and new friends were introduced. A happy, chaotic place, full of joy and celebration.

Except for *this* particular festival.

For the bards awoke this morning to hear that their beloved High Bard had died in the night. Laughter has turned to tears, singing has turned to mourning, and the festival itself has become a funeral.

Nixha comes for all rabbits, and every song or story or poem has to end. The High Bard's time of telling tales has finished. The bards will ensure that his words go on and that he becomes a part of them.

But first, it is time to say goodbye.

Smoke

—⁓—

W hy are you crying?"

The bard and his little apprentice, Rue, are standing next to the stones of Blackhenge, looking down into a valley filled with tents, stages, and flagpoles. The morning sun is glinting on the volcanic glass of the stones, the sky is pure forget-me-not blue, and tiny butterflies flit to and fro among the flowers. It seems like the perfect start to the perfect day.

And yet the bard is struggling to hold back giant, tearful sobs. His mouth is clenched, his fists bunched, his body literally shakes with the effort, but his eyes have betrayed him: tears have soaked his face; they roll down his nose and drip onto his cloak.

"What's making you so sad?" Rue has never seen the

old rabbit like this. He clutches at the bard's breeches, feeling like crying himself. Unable to speak, the bard points down toward the festival below. It was supposed to be a celebration: the annual get-together of bards from all over the Five Realms to swap songs, stories, and sagas. Now it is a funeral instead.

The centerpiece of the gathering had been a large hexagonal stage. Just last night they had been sitting around it, watching performers weave their magic over the audience. The wooden boards have now been hacked to pieces to build a funeral pyre, upon which the body of the High Bard has been laid, draped in rainbow flags, bunting, and garlands of daffodils. From what Rue can gather, he died in the night, sending the whole festival into mourning.

All the bards have gathered around the pyre. They have dressed themselves in their brightest outfits, tied colored pennants to their staves, even dyed their fur in vibrant streaks of orange, violet, and spring green. From up on the hillside it looks like several rainbows have collided, shattering into a puddle of shards, to fill the valley below.

Rue stares at the sight, scratching his ear. "I thought people wear black when someone dies," he says. "It looks like they're having a party."

"He . . . he always . . . hated black," the bard manages to say before the sobs threaten to overtake him again. There is a flare as someone lights the pyre, and flames begin to lick over the piled wood. The rainbow flags start to blacken and shrivel.

"Did you know him, then?" Rue asks. He can't understand why his master is so upset about someone they had only seen on the stage.

"Very . . . well," says the bard.

Smoke is drifting up from the pyre now. The stack of wood has been packed with incense and herbs. Even though they stand high above, Rue can catch a hint of the scent: patchouli and lavender. Sweet, white smoke rising up to drift away in the breeze.

"Then why aren't we down there with everyone else?" The bard had dragged him out of bed at first light, and Rue had been looking forward to another day of exploring the festival. It seems unfair that they are missing out, even if it is a sad occasion.

"Because," is all the bard says. He reaches out a paw, as if to touch the smoke that is lazily curling up out of the valley. Rue thinks he hears him whisper "Goodbye," and then the bard turns to walk away, pulling Rue along beside him.

⸺◦⸺

They march eastward for the rest of the morning, along the top of the downs, the bard keeping up a fast pace that has Rue panting for breath. The little rabbit has a ton of questions but no time to ask them (which he suspects is a cunning plan on the bard's part). The questions bubble up inside him, making him hop and skip as he walks. When the rabbits finally stop for a rest, out the questions come, one after another like an overflowing teapot.

"So how do you know the High Bard? How did he die? Why did we have to leave so soon? Is it something to do with your real name? What is your real name? Why won't you tell me? Where are we going now?"

The bard sinks to the ground, stretches out his legs, groans, then lies back on the spongy heather, looking up at the pure blue, endless sky.

"Are you ignoring me? Why are you ignoring me? Is it because I ask too many questions? Is it? Is it?"

The bard stays silent but pats the spot of ground next to him. With a sigh, Rue drops his stick and pack and lies down next to his master.

"If I tell you why we had to leave, do you promise to stay quiet for five minutes?" the bard asks. Rue can't help noticing that the bard's voice sounds strained and a bit husky.

"I'll try," Rue says.

"As I said, I knew the High Bard well. When I was younger. He was like a father to me, once. My own father died when I was very young."

"How?" Rue asks, then bites his tongue, hoping he hasn't ruined the flow of information he was finally getting.

"Never you mind," says the bard. "Anyway, the High Bard—although he was just an ordinary bard back then—raised me and taught me all the art I know. I would have loved to be there by the pyre, singing songs and telling tales about him, but it's too dangerous."

"Dangerous?" Rue sits up and stares at his master. "Do you mean with the fire and the patchouli and everything?"

"No," says the bard. "Dangerous because people are looking for me. Bad people. That's why I have to keep my hood down, and why I can't tell anybody who I am."

"Why are they looking for you? What have you done?" Rue can't help a touch of morbid excitement creeping into his voice.

"Nothing *that* interesting," says the bard. "I just told the wrong story to the wrong people, that's all."

"Are the ones looking for you wearing black cloaks?" Rue asks. "With swords underneath?"

"They might be," says the bard. He reaches out to squeeze Rue's arm. "Why? Did you see someone like that? Someone watching us at the festival?"

"No," says Rue. "Not at the festival."

"It was just something you imagined, then," says the bard, breathing a sigh of relief.

"Not really," says Rue. He lifts a finger and points back along the downs. "There's one over there, watching us right now."

"What?" The bard jumps up, staring westward, where, sure enough, a lone figure stands a hundred feet away, motionless. A hooded somebody with black robes gently flapping in the slight breeze. The bard spots a sword sheath and a gray-furred paw lightly resting on the hilt.

"Whiskers!" he curses, grabbing his pack and staff. He turns to run east, but there—on the path ahead—stand two more figures, identical to the first. There's no escape in any direction, just the steep edges of the downs falling away on either side, where they would quickly stumble and be caught.

"We're trapped, aren't we?" says Rue, his lip beginning to tremble.

"I'm sorry," is all the bard can reply, and he sinks to the ground again, waiting for the strangers' unstoppable approach.

———

As he sits among the chalk and heather, listening to the slowly approaching footsteps of his assassins, the bard looks out at the spectacular view. From up here, on the spine of the Razorback Downs, the whole of Grimheart

Forest spreads out all the way to the horizon. An unbroken ocean of green leaves in every possible shade.

Funny, he thinks. *I've been terrified of this moment for over a year. But now that it's here, I don't really mind that much.*

It is true — if anything, he feels quite peaceful. The worst thing imaginable is about to happen, and there is nothing he can do to stop it. All that worry, fear, and tension is now over. Of course, he will miss his friends: little Rue, his sister, and his brother.

Podkin. He won't get to see him again after all. He really should have stayed at Thornwood a bit longer. Hugged him a bit tighter when he left . . .

Still, there is nothing he can do about it now.

He stares at the forest again. All the times he has spent there, all those adventures. And now here he is, about to be struck dead, and yet everything will carry on just as normal underneath the leaves and branches, in the cool, mossy darkness of the forest world.

The bard sighs and wraps one of Rue's little paws in his own, squeezing tight. The cloaked assassins are here now. The footsteps halt, and Rue gives a gasp of surprise.

"Look!" he says. "They've got masks made of bone! Are they bonedancers, like Zarza from the story you told me?"

The bard looks up at the three figures that now surround him. They have black hooded cloaks and long robes.

Beneath their cowls, sunlight gleams on polished bone carved with whorls, spirals, and runes. From the holes in their masks, three pairs of eyes watch him: cold, calm, emotionless.

"Yes," says the bard. "They're bonedancers. You don't need to sound quite so excited, though. They *have* come to kill me."

One of the cloaked figures reaches into its robe. The bard's calm feelings from a few moments ago suddenly evaporate.

"Wait," he says. "Before you do it — please don't let the boy see. And there are some gems in my bag. They're yours, if you would just take him back to the festival for me . . . you know . . . afterward . . . and make sure there's someone to look after him. He's my apprentice, you see. He needs to learn the ways —"

"I'm your apprentice?" Rue almost jumps out of his fur. The bard remembers he hasn't told the boy about his discussion with the High Bard yet. He probably should have mentioned it, but the funeral . . .

"Drink this," says the bonedancer, bringing a glass vial out of her robe instead of the knife the bard was expecting. "Don't worry about the boy."

"Poison?" says the bard. "I thought that was more the style of the Shadow Clans of Hulstland. Have you lot stopped using blades, then?"

"Drink it," says the bonedancer.

Uncorking the vial, the bard takes a sniff. Valerian, a hint of poppy seed. It smells more like a sleeping draft than something deadly.

"Don't do it!" Rue shouts, eyes brimming with tears.

The bard puts a hand on his shoulder. "Relax," he says. "If there's one thing I've learned in all my years, it's never to argue with three deadly assassins who could chop you into twenty pieces before you even have time to blink."

Before Rue can stop him, he glugs down the mixture. It tastes bitter, makes his mouth go numb. He thinks there might be a touch of magnolia in it too, some lavender, maybe . . .

. . . and then he is gone.

CHAPTER TWO

Spinestone

———

The first thing the bard feels is a gentle rocking motion, interrupted every now and then by an unpleasant bump. He is lying on his back, with a hard wooden surface beneath him, and it seems as though someone has stuffed his head full of angora wool.

He can hear the slow creak of wood grinding against wood and the *scratch-scratch* of animal paws on packed earth. Behind those sounds, there is the rustling of reeds, the tooting call of marsh birds — coots, he thinks — and the high-pitched whine of mosquitoes swarming everywhere.

I'm not dead yet, then, he thinks. *On a wagon, though. Being taken somewhere.*

He has a good idea of where that might be and opens

14

one eye to check. Things are a bit blurry, but he can make out the little shape of Rue — sitting, clutching his cloak — the sides of the wagon, some silhouettes that are probably the bonedancers, and above him a wide, pink-tinted sky. The sun is just beginning to set.

"You're awake!" Rue shouts, almost jumping on his chest.

"Are you all right?" the bard manages to say, his words slurring and muddling together. "Have they hurt you?"

"No, they haven't. I'm fine. The sisters have been really nice to me. We all carried you down the hill, and then they found this farmer with a wagon and made him give us a ride. I think he was crying, and he might have wet himself a bit. They're taking us to —"

"Spinestone," the bard finishes Rue's sentence. *Spinestone. The temple warren of the bonedancers.* Not a place the bard has ever really wanted to see. They haven't killed him already because they are taking him back to their home to do it properly.

As if to confirm his fears, one of the bonedancers moves to his side, peering down at him through the holes in her mask.

"Why did you have to drug me?" the bard asks. "I would have come quietly."

"Just to be sure," says the bonedancer. "You have been a difficult target for us to find."

"You didn't put my apprentice to sleep."

"He is a good boy," says the bonedancer. She reaches out to ruffle Rue's ears, and he smiles back at her.

Traitorous little weasel, the bard thinks.

"We are nearly there," the bonedancer continues. "You should try to sit up."

With some help, they manage to get the bard into a sitting position. His head and vision are slowly clearing, and he can make out the wagon, the trembling farmer driving it, and the two brown rats pulling it along a narrow track. On either side of the road, swampy marshland stretches into the distance. Up ahead, bursting through the reeds, is a huge ridge of stone, shattered and spiked at the top into a crest of shards that looks like the backbone of a colossal fallen monster. Underneath it, he knows, the bonedancers have lived, worshiped, and trained for centuries. The sight of it makes his insides tighten into a knot of dread.

"Now that you've got me," he manages to say, "I don't suppose you can tell me who it is that has paid for me to be killed? I'm pretty sure I know, but I'd like to be certain."

"You will find out soon enough," says the bonedancer, turning back to her sisters and leaving the bard to watch Spinestone getting closer and closer.

⌇

They draw up outside the gates and clamber out of the wagon, leaving the terrified farmer to gallop away as fast as his rats can go. The bard and Rue gasp as they look up at the two enormous statues flanking the giant double-doored entrance, both of them carved out of the granite hillside. As terrified as he is about being killed, the bard can't help but be impressed at the sight.

The statue on the left is a graceful doe rabbit dressed in a long robe with a belt of skulls. She holds a bow in one hand; the other rests on the quiver of arrows at her side. "Nixha," says the bard, pointing. "The goddess of death and sister of Estra. She is worshiped by the bonedancers."

"Who's the other one?" Rue asks. The statue on the right is a masked rabbit holding a two-handed sword with a strange, backward-curved blade.

"That must be Cero," says the bard. "The first bone-dancer. She was once a princess, about to be married against her will to the prince of the neighboring warren. But it was all a trick. When her tribe invited her groom-to-be and his family into their longburrow, the visitors came in, pulled out their weapons, attacked everyone, and stole all their treasure."

"Did she die?" Rue asks.

"No, she survived. But only her. Then she went away and learned how to fight. How to fight *really* well."

"Did she have her revenge on the nasty groom?"

"I'll say," says the bard. "She chopped the whole warren up so small they had to be buried in buckets. Nixha saw it all, as the story goes, and was so impressed she told Cero to come here and train more rabbits like her to be the goddess's servants. I'll tell you the tale properly one day." The bard gulps loudly, then adds, "Hopefully."

Two of the bonedancers now place their hands on the bard's shoulders, moving him forward. The third waves up at the entrance, signaling to someone inside, and the doors begin to creak open. Under the cold stone gaze of Nixha and her servant, the bard and Rue are marched into the temple.

—◊◊◊—

Rue gapes as they enter. The little rabbit has never seen anything constructed on this scale, and never with so much stone.

The doors open onto a wide entrance tunnel built of carved granite, with a gleaming polished marble floor. Oil lamps line the walls, making everything shine much brighter than in most rabbit warrens. The ceiling is very high, sculpted into arches and ridges, with a few too many skull motifs for the bard's liking. Tapestries hang everywhere, all done in black and white, and all showing various scenes of Nixha taking lives. Mostly with her bow, sometimes with swords, knives, axes ... even a pitchfork. The bard begins to sweat uncontrollably.

"Look at all the bonedancers!" Rue whispers. The bard has noticed them too, although he is not as excited about it as his apprentice. The masked, robed sisters are everywhere, silently moving across the shiny floor like a troupe of ice skaters. They wear black robes, gray robes, some with a silver trim. There are even some rabbits in white with unmasked faces.

"Who are they?" Rue asks, finding it impossible not to gape at everything.

"Initiates," replies the bard. "Those who have just joined the order. They haven't earned their masks yet."

"You know a lot about us for one who has never been to Spinestone before," says one of the bonedancers behind him. The bard swallows hard.

"I have had some experience with your order," he says. "In a good way, of course," he quickly adds.

"What's in that room, there?" Rue is pointing through an archway at a chamber that seems to be filled with tall piles of mud.

"The termite mounds," answers one of their escorts.

"Termites?" says Rue, stopping to stare for a second before he is nudged onward again.

"Bonedancers have to kill something every day," says

21

the bard. "It's part of their tradition, remember? They carry pouches of bugs around with them, so it doesn't *always* have to be a rabbit."

Both he and Rue look at the waists of the bonedancers behind them, spotting the leather pouches next to their sheathed swords. Rue wishes he could see them kill a bug. The bard prays they have done today's kill already.

"The Hall of Trials," says one of their escorts. The bard and Rue look up as they enter a wide circular chamber, its ceiling the bare jagged stone of the hill itself. It is lit by an enormous chandelier, and stark, angular shadows are cast all around its edges — zigs and zags of overlapping darkness.

Pillars ring the Hall's edge, and in between them are more black-and-white tapestries hanging from ceiling to floor. Each bears a skull-like bonedancer mask, repeated over and over. Although, looking closer, the bard realizes the patterns on each mask are subtly different.

They walk past a deep pit set into the polished marble floor. Peering into it, the bard sees bones strewn all over its bottom, and the grille of a cage on one wall. For a second, he is certain he spots a pair of glowing eyes behind it, accompanied by a low chittering sound, but when he looks again, it is gone.

He half expects to feel a shove from behind at any

moment, sending him down into the pit—dinner for the half-starved giant stoat or weasel they probably keep in there—but they march on, up to the far edge of the hall. There, partly draped in shadow, is a raised throne decorated with carved skulls of every size. Sitting on it is a bonedancer, an old one, dressed in black robes with scarlet trim and with a mask almost completely covered in silver swirls. A single red ruby shines on her forehead, and the eyes beneath it are a cold, cold blue. They watch, unblinking, as the bard and Rue are brought close.

"Probably a good idea to kneel," the bard whispers to Rue, and they both sink down to their knees, waiting for the bonedancer on the throne to speak.

"You are Wulf the Wanderer," she says finally. It is a statement, not a question, and although her voice is cracked with age, you can still hear the strength underneath.

"Yes, ma'am," says the bard, bowing his hooded head.

"I am no madam," says the bonedancer. "I am Mother Superior. But you may address me by my official name: Sythica." She points a white-furred finger at Rue. "Who is this?"

"My apprentice, ma—Sythica," says the bard. "Perhaps he could just be allowed to leave? He has nothing to do with this business."

"We know that." Sythica turns her attention to the bard

again. "You are aware we have been offered a payment for your death?"

"I am." The bard swallows hard, thinking of the weasel pit behind him and how painful it might be to get eaten alive.

"And you know what you have done to warrant this?"

"I think so," says the bard. "I told the wrong story in the wrong warren, I presume?"

"You did," says Sythica. "At Golden Brook. At the chieftain's wedding celebrations, no less. And it was a story involving us, was it not?"

The bard winces. "Your order had a small part in it, yes."

Sythica nods. "It is for that reason we have decided not to carry out your execution." The bard's heart skips a beat, until Sythica fixes her cold eyes on him again. "Yet."

"Yet?" he asks.

"Yes," says Sythica. "We wish to hear this story that has earned you a contract on your life. You will tell it to us, exactly as you told it to the Golden Brook rabbits. We will judge whether it is offensive enough for you to die, and if the goddess Nixha demands it, then die you shall."

"And if she quite likes the tale?"

"Then you may go free."

The bard clears his throat in order to begin talking, but Sythica gestures to the bonedancers behind him. They hoist him up to his feet again.

"You will perform in the morning," says Sythica. "Until then, you are our guests."

"That's nice," says Rue as the bonedancers march them out of the chamber. "I've never been anyone's guest before."

"I think she means 'guest' as in 'prisoner,'" says the bard, although he doesn't feel too bad about it. He has been given a chance not only to save his life, but to do it by telling a story.

And telling stories is what he does best.

They are taken out of the hall, down a side burrow, and into a simple cell. It has bare stone walls, two wooden cots, a washstand, and a table set out with a simple supper of lettuce leaves and diced carrots. While they stand there, looking at their surroundings, the bonedancers leave, shutting the door behind them. There is a loud click as it is locked.

Prisoners.

Rue grabs a handful of lettuce and shoves it into his mouth, asking questions while he is crunching, spraying bits of half-chomped salad down his front. "Are they really going to kill you? What story did you tell? Didn't Podkin meet a rabbit from Golden Brook Warren?"

"Vetch," says the bard. The last story he'd told Rue was about how Podkin rescued the sacred hammer of Applecross, meeting some new rabbits along the way. A bonedancer called Zarza, a bard called Yarrow, and Vetch —a rabbit from the richest warren in Gotland.

"Yes, him," says Rue. "Was your story about him? The Golden Brook rabbits must have *really* hated it if they want to kill you for it. Who under earth could hate a story so much? They're supposed to be fun."

"Some stories are told for fun," says the bard. "Some stories are told to pass on lessons. Some are told to help people think, and *some . . .* some are told to show people the truth. Not everybody likes being told the truth."

Rue frowns for a moment and is about to launch into another volley of questions, but the bard has made his way over to one of the cots. His head is still groggy from the sleeping potion, and now that his impending death seems to have been put on pause, his bones feel as heavy as the granite rock all around him. He collapses on the bed, asleep within seconds, and no amount of whisker pulling or ear flicking can wake him.

———

Some hours later, the cell door is unlocked with a loud clank and two white-robed initiates bustle in, refill the oil lamps, place jugs of water on the washstand, and leave a breakfast of porridge on the table. They are gone again before Rue opens his eyes properly. From his tangled nest of blankets, he sees the bard, already up, sitting cross-legged on his bed with his eyes closed.

"About time you were awake," the bard says. "Get yourself some porridge. We've got a long day ahead."

"What are you doing?" asks Rue, yawning and trying to untangle himself. A whole bed without any brothers in it is a luxury to him, and he doesn't feel like leaving it just yet.

"Unraveling the story," says the bard, his eyes still closed. "It's been coiled up in my memory warren and needs straightening out before I tell it."

Rue remembers Yarrow, the bard from the last tale, talking about a "memory warren." The place where he stored all his stories and poems.

"You've never done that before."

"I've never had to save my life with a story before," says the bard. "At least, not since that unfortunate incident with the giant rabbits in Orestad." He opens one eye to look at Rue. "Never tell a giant rabbit the tale of 'Jen and the Beanstalk.' I learned that the hard way."

Rue just has time to gulp down a bowl of buttery, oaty porridge before the cell door opens again. This time, three masked bonedancers are there, ready to escort them back to the hall.

"Off we go!" says the bard, hopping down from his bed. His eyes shine bright green, and Rue notices he has repainted the blue swirls on his fur with fresh dye. *He's actually looking forward to this,* thinks the little rabbit. *He isn't scared at all!* Rue himself is terrified, and he's not the one with his life at stake.

Gazing at his master with newfound wonder, Rue follows him out of the cell and down the tunnel.

—⁓—

The Hall of Trials has changed overnight. Tiers of benches have been brought in, turning the place into a kind of amphitheater. The seats are filled with row upon row of bonedancers, all sitting motionless and impassive, like a collection of carvings. Rue estimates three hundred or more: probably every occupant of Spinestone. Enough assassins to kill the whole of the Five Realms.

There is a raised wooden dais in the hall's center, ready for the bard to stand and tell his story. Rue notices that it backs onto the pit, from which a gnawing and squeaking can be heard. *That doesn't bode well,* he thinks, but the bard doesn't seem to notice. He strides onto the stage and stands proud, looking around at his audience and smiling.

It's all a show, Rue realizes as he is led to a space in the front row. *This confidence must be part of the act. Who would believe a story from a stuttering, shivering bard?* Even so, to stand there, unarmed, unprotected, in front of the scariest collection of killers in the Five Realms, with nothing but a tale to save you ... the bard must have whiskers of solid steel.

"Good morning, bard," comes the clear voice of Sythica. "I believe you have a story for us."

The bard bows elaborately to the imposing figure on the throne before him. "I do indeed, Your Excellency. Shall I begin?"

"Please do."

Rue watches every faceless mask turn to the bard. Three hundred cold, merciless stares. Three hundred priestesses of death who have yet to kill their daily victim. He swallows hard and mutters a prayer to the Goddess, then another to Clarion, god of bards ...

Please let it be a good story ... Please let them like it ...

"Well," says the bard, "this is the tale I told at Golden Brook Warren. The tale that might possibly get me killed. It is the true story of a legendary battle. One that you might have heard of. The Battle of Sparrowfast ..."

The Tale Begins

L
ike a square of a patchwork quilt, as many stories are, this tale is just a piece of a bigger one, but I hope it's entertaining all the same (unless, of course, you happen to be from Golden Brook).

All rabbits have heard of Podkin One-Ear and his struggle against the Gorm. All rabbits remember those dark days when warriors wrapped in poisoned iron marched out of the north and tried to wrench the whole Five Realms apart so that their god, Gormalech, could consume it all.

Young Podkin, his family, and his friends had already started to fight back against that evil. They had rescued Surestrike, the hammer of Applecross, and used it to forge three Gormkiller arrows. They had found Moonfyre, the lost brooch, and saved the dagger Starclaw. With Ailfew, the magic sickle of Redwater, taking their tally of Gifts to four, they had found a home at Dark Hollow Warren, deep in Grimheart Forest, and were planning their next move.

They were a ragtag bunch of soldiers, farmers, and survivors from all the Gorm-ravaged lands. They had escaped by the skin of their ears, come through a tough, snowy winter, and were not yet safe by any means. The Gorm were still about; the Gorm could still find them. What could a tatty, helpless rabble do against such a hopeless threat?

Podkin and his big sister, Paz, were on the war council, helping to make those very decisions. It was something Podkin had wanted for a long time, but he was still only eight summers old, and he was finding all the long meetings and discussions a bit hard to follow.

There were so many different personalities and different ideas to listen to. Crom, the blind veteran warrior, was strong yet cautious. Rill, the shield-maiden, was fierce and keen for war. Dodge, the gray rabbit from Muggy Pit Warren, was all for fleeing, and Rowan, the sable-furred councilor, changed her mind like the wind. Between them all, it was difficult to decide on what to have for breakfast, let alone how to defeat the Gorm.

In the meantime, their warren was steadily growing.

Podkin's first idea as councilor had been to send out Mish and Mash, the acrobatic dwarf rabbits, to find all the refugees and survivors who had been eking out a living on the forest's edge.

They had been very successful in discovering little makeshift scrapes and shelters and bringing their occupants back. The number of rabbits at Dark Hollow had swelled throughout the spring. Forty, then fifty, and now sixty or more rabbits were living in the warren, making it almost as noisy and bustling as the homes they had all been forced from in the months past.

Feeding and caring for all those mouths was not an easy task, and being partly in charge of it all had opened Podkin's eyes to just how difficult a chieftain's job must be. He often thought of his father, killed by Scramashank the Gorm Lord, and marveled at how he had made the whole thing look so easy.

Paz, on the other hand, seemed to be taking to it like a duck to water, which Podkin found most annoying.

"What about a night attack?" Rill said one morning at a council meeting. "We could use Moonfyre to jump into a Gorm camp, shoot Scramashank with the arrows, and then jump out again."

"Not a good idea," said Paz. "We'd have to know where their camp was, for a start; then we'd have to know if Scramashank was actually there. We'd have to have a decent bow to fire the arrows, and Podkin would have to be the one doing the jumping, which wouldn't be safe."

"I've done worse than that before," Podkin said, puffing out his little chest. "I'm not scared."

"I'm sure Mother wouldn't agree to it," said Paz with a flick of her ears.

Podkin looked across the longburrow to where his mother was sitting, helping some other rabbits patch armor and sharpen weapons. They had rescued her from the Gorm last winter, and she had spent a long time in an awful sleeping sickness. It was so good to have her back with them, but unfortunately she was making up for lost time by trying to wrap Podkin up in angora wool and keep him out of each and every danger.

"It's not up to her," said Podkin, not sounding very convincing.

"Well, I wouldn't want to be the one to argue with her," said Crom. The other council rabbits nodded their heads and made frightened noises.

Great, Podkin thought. *I've faced off the Gorm Lord twice, fought my way through all sorts of impending doom, and now everybody's worried about what my mother might say.*

"If we're not going to attack," said Rill, thankfully changing the subject, "then what's the point of us being here? We can't just hide in the forest and wait for them to go away."

"We will strike," said Crom. "But the time has to be right. We need more allies, more weapons."

"Which we will find in the lands to the south," said Dodge. "We must leave for Thrianta or Orestad, places the Gorm haven't yet reached."

Here we go again, Podkin thought. Their daily discussions just seemed to go around and around in circles. He desperately wanted to come up with a genius idea that everyone agreed with, but his brain remained empty no matter how hard he racked it. *Maybe I shouldn't have been included on the council after all.* He had been thinking that more and more lately. If only the Goddess would pop an answer into his head so he could prove his worth. He muttered another little prayer, but it didn't seem to do any good.

The sound of the warren doors booming echoed down the entrance tunnel, interrupting the meeting (much to Podkin's relief). Then came running feet, chattering voices, and then Mish and Mash burst into the room, accompanied by the brown-and-green-clad rabbits who made up their scouting party.

"Gorm!" Mash shouted. "At the forest's edge!"

"That's nothing new," said Crom. "They've been patrolling there for months."

"This isn't a patrol," said Mish. "It's an army. And they're here to destroy the forest."

This last statement drew everyone's attention, and soon there was a crowd of rabbits around the scouts, all asking questions at once. Voices grew louder and louder, attracting more and more rabbits to add to the hubbub until there was so much noise that —

"Quiet, everyone!"

Crom had his mouth open, ready to shout, but the bellow that silenced the longburrow had come from Lady Enna, Podkin's mother. All eyes turned to Crom in shock, as the whole burrow had become used to him taking the lead. How would he react to someone else stealing his thunder? Was there going to be some kind of fight?

There was a beat or two of silence; then the blind warrior simply shrugged. Eyebrows were raised and ears twitched, but Podkin himself wasn't too surprised. He knew Crom had no interest in running the warren anyway. It could have been Crom's if he'd wanted it back when Crom's father died, but Crom had chosen a different path. He would still be on it, too, if Podkin hadn't met him in Boneroot all those months ago.

Lady Enna wasn't surprised either. She was more than used to getting her own way. "Now," she said to Mish and Mash, "go on with your report, please."

"Well," said Mish, "we were out looking for more refugees, not far from the forest edge, when we heard this horrific sound —"

"Grinding and tearing," said Mash. "Screeching and cracking and wailing."

"So we crept closer to investigate," Mish continued. "We poked our noses out of the trees and saw them down by the crater, where Boneroot used to be."

"Gorm," said Mash. "More than I've ever seen before. But this time, they had something with them."

"Big wheely, turny things," said Mish. "With blades and knives and choppy bits. They were using them to pull up trees, and crunch them and smash them."

"Wheely, turny things?" Yarrow the bard spoke up. He was obviously collecting snippets for his epic yarn about the Gorm. "Could you describe them in a bit more detail? Do a little sketch, perhaps?"

"A sketch? They're ripping up the whole forest!" Mash finished, pulling his own ears in fright. "There's going to be nothing left but mud and splinters soon! This isn't the time for doodling!"

"I think you'll find there's always time for doodling, dear," Yarrow said, making the little rabbit hop up and down with rage.

"Calm down, calm down," said Crom, stepping up to put a soothing hand on Mash's shoulder. "Grimheart is the biggest forest in the Five Realms. It's not going anywhere, whatever the Gorm do to it."

"Why are they tearing it down?" Paz asked. "Are they looking for us?"

"Ridiculous," said Lady Enna. "Surely they would just walk in if they were."

Podkin sometimes forgot his mother had been asleep, on the brink of death, for so long. She had missed out on lots of things they had discovered about their enemy.

"The Gorm are scared of the forest, Mother," he said. "It belongs to Hern the Hunter. They don't like to come in here. That's what's kept us safe this long."

"Yes," agreed Brigid. The witch-rabbit had joined the throng and was nodding in that knowing way of hers. "But they've worked out a way to get to us. Their metal machinery can tear down our hiding place and weaken Hern at the same time. It's another blow against the Balance and will help them grow in power. Two berries on one branch."

Podkin remembered Brigid telling him about the Balance: the ancient agreement between the goddesses and Gormalech that kept each side in check. The Gorm were trying to destroy it so their god could take over the world again.

"I think we need to get a good idea of what they're up to," said Crom. "Mish and Mash can take some councilors out for a better look."

"I'll go," said Rill immediately.

"Me too," said Podkin. This was his chance to do something worthwhile as part of the council. He'd spied on the Gorm lots of times before, and it was much more interesting than sitting in a meeting.

"No, you jolly well won't," said his mother, crossing her arms. Podkin sighed. He really wished she would stop being so protective. If she'd seen half the things he'd done while she was asleep . . .

"I'll go with him, Mother," said Paz. "My sickle will keep us safe. I can grow leaves and branches around us so the Gorm won't see us."

"Both of you? Never! Next you'll be saying you're taking your baby brother, Pook, as well!"

Podkin didn't want to mention that Pook had been in several near-death scrapes alongside them over the past few months. Instead he decided to try a different tactic.

"Brigid will tell you it's fine for us to go. If anything bad was going to happen to us, she'd know already."

Brigid was a soothsayer, who knew things before they took place. She was also the only rabbit in Dark Hollow whom Lady Enna would listen to, probably because the old witch-rabbit had saved her life. Everyone turned to look at her, but she just twitched her ears.

"I haven't had any signs that they shouldn't go," she said finally.

"Great. That's settled, then." Podkin grabbed Paz's arm and pulled her toward their room, where their cloaks and packs were stored. Their mother might have argued further, but Pook was scrabbling at her robes and asking for soup, and the babble of questions for Mish and Mash had started again. If they were quick, they could get out of the warren and away before their mother could do anything about it.

"Who'd have thought we'd actually be running *toward* the Gorm for once?" Paz said as they dashed into their room and began tying on their cloaks.

"Just goes to show how dull council meetings are," said Podkin, but he, too, was surprised. Not long ago, he had been living in constant fear of their iron-clad enemies. Now he couldn't wait to be doing something about them again.

He hoped he wouldn't regret being so keen.

—◦—

Within half an hour, a small group had gathered outside the warren doors. There was Podkin and Paz, Mish and Mash, Rill the shield-maiden, and Yarrow the bard. The descriptions of Gorm war machines had sounded too intriguing for him to miss out on.

They were all dressed in shades of brown and green, with long hooded cloaks. Mish and Mash were adding some extra fern fronds and vines of ivy for camouflage.

"Do I have to be draped in this stuff?" Podkin asked as a fat spider dropped from the greenery on his head and scuttled across his shoulder. "I do know how to hide from enemies, thank you very much."

"Stop whining," said Paz. "It could be worse." She closed her eyes for a moment and drew on the power of Ailfew. The ivy on Podkin's hood began to grow, twining itself around his head like a crown.

"Stop it!" he shouted, clawing the stuff off. *Paz and her turnipping sickle.* He wished one of his Gifts had a power that could get back at her, but his brooch worked only in the light of the moon, and his dagger would slice her into bits. That would be a bit extreme.

"Knock it off, you two," said Mish. "We've got a long way to go, and you can't be bickering the whole time."

With everyone ready, they set off into the forest at a jog.

When they had first arrived at Dark Hollow — frozen, starving, and scared — the trees of Grimheart had seemed thick and impenetrable. But in the past months, the scouts had been hard at work, and now there was a network of paths spreading out from the warren in all directions.

The paths had been marked with symbols carved into bark here and there. Some led to spots where they could forage for mushrooms, nuts, or berries; some led to lookout posts or other warrens. Mish and Mash read them easily, and even Crom could feel them with his fingers, allowing him to find his way around the woods without help.

Summer was now in full swing, which also helped to make the forest seem more pleasant. Dark green leaves rustled overhead, birdsong echoed between the trees from all directions, and the air was filled with buzzing, flittering insects and drifting seedpods, all glinting and sparkling as they passed through slanting beams of light.

I'm turning into a forest rabbit, Podkin thought as he wove his way in and out of roots and trunks. The quiet hum of life around him, the shelter and solidity of the trees — it all made him feel safe and protected, almost as if Hern himself were looking after him. Were the Gorm really powerful enough to destroy all this?

They stopped at lunchtime for a quick meal of dandelion leaves and acorn bread, and then they were off again, following Mish and Mash as they darted from path to path.

Podkin found he could only just keep up with the twin rabbits. Paz was also struggling, and poor Yarrow was lagging farther and farther behind, muttering things about suffering for his art and how everyone had better like his saga.

Even at that pace, it was early evening before they began to near the edge of the great forest.

That was when they heard the noise.

Podkin tried to describe it later but found he had no words. Even Yarrow was hard-pressed doing justice to how awful it was.

It started as a low rumbling that shook the trees all around them. As they got closer to it, they could hear screeching metal and distant crashes. Nearer still, and they could hear crunching, grinding, and tearing, and finally they heard moans and screams of terrified, tortured creatures.

They were at the forest edge now, where the trees were younger and thinner. Bramble bushes, heavy with ripening blackberries, filled the gaps between the young oaks, rowans, and elms. Dodging through these, they crept forward, trying to get a glimpse of just what could be making such a hideous racket.

Podkin was the first to see it, and, when he did, he drew a sharp breath. Paz did the same, while Rill muttered a soldier's curse that would have made even Crom's whiskers curl.

"By Clarion's sacred harp strings," whispered Yarrow. Their eyes were all wide, their mouths open. Even knowing firsthand how evil the Gorm could be, nothing could have prepared them for *this*.

They had emerged from the trees a hundred yards or

so from the crater where Boneroot Warren had once been hidden. The giant hole was clearly visible, and on the far side of it were the Gorm.

Podkin had seen as many as fifty together before, but here there were far more. A hundred at least, their hulking iron forms easy to identify. But it wasn't the number of them that shocked him, rather it was what they were doing to the forest.

Mash was right when he spoke about mud and splinters. The Gorm were tearing the whole place down.

At the front of their line, half hidden by the forest itself, were ten contraptions built from the same rusted, jagged iron as the Gorm's armor. Like some kind of awful giant insects, they had an array of blades — spinning teeth and crushing jaws — at the front. At the back, each had a massive wheel, taller than five rabbits, which spun steadily around, powering the cutting equipment before them.

The constructs were being pushed by teams of Gorm and driven into the trees and bushes. The blades tore through trunks and roots, iron mandibles crushed and chomped branches into pieces, and teeth crunched wood into splinters. Behind them was a swath of torn-up ground. Piles of gouged mud and pieces of tree were everywhere, and the trail stretched back half a mile or more.

The devastation was awful, and it was made worse by the fires. Teams of giant rats were pulling the fallen trees toward colossal bonfires to be burned. Centuries upon centuries' worth of growth was being eaten up by the walls of flame and rising into the sky in pillars of ash that must have been visible for miles around.

The smoke, mixed with the stink of grinding iron and ripped-up earth, stung the rabbits' eyes and caught in their throats.

"Now do you see what I mean?" said Mash. "The whole forest will soon be gone. They're tearing through it so fast!"

"Why?" Podkin managed to say. "Why do this? Just to get at us? Do they really hate us that much?"

"Well, you did chop off the Gorm Lord's foot," Paz said. "And you cut Surestrike out of his hand. He'd probably grind down the whole Five Realms to get his revenge."

"What makes those . . . things . . . move?" asked Rill, peering at the iron juggernauts. "Is there something inside the wheels?"

Podkin looked closer, trying to spot what was making the wheels turn. There was definitely something living inside them. He could see Gorm handlers swinging barbed whips at them and yelling. Some had spears, which they were prodding between the spokes. His first thought was rats, until he glimpsed an arm poking from the nearest machine. A rabbit arm, stretching out for mercy.

46

"By the Goddess," Podkin said, his voice choking. "They've got *rabbits* in there."

Judging by the horror on Mish's and Mash's faces, they hadn't noticed that fact before. Rill was shaking her head, and Paz was quietly crying. Yarrow just stared at the scene, not even blinking, before he finally spoke.

"I've heard stories before, horrible ones, about a place called Hell, where all the evil of the world lives. I thought they were just fables, made up to terrify little rabbit kittens. Now I know what Hell must look like."

Podkin wasn't listening. He had spotted something else down there, among the fire and torn wood. One of the Gorm wasn't poking slaves, pushing machines, or feeding the bonfires. It was just standing there, hands on hips, rocking back and forth with what looked like laughter. It was taller than the others and had mismatched horns of iron curving up from its head. One of its feet was a jagged mass of iron shards, and rabbit skulls hung from its belt.

Even though he had faced that Gorm twice before and bested him, Podkin felt his blood run cold.

Scramashank. The Gorm Lord, who had killed his father and hounded Podkin across the country. He was here, causing all this devastation. And he was actually *enjoying* it.

Podkin ducked back into the forest, pulling Paz after him, and started to run for home.

Leaving

~⁓~

Back at Dark Hollow, they were huddled around a map of the forest, spread out across one of the longburrow benches and marked with carved wooden pieces to represent their warren and the approaching Gorm. The whole council was present; also Yarrow, Brigid, Podkin's mother, and even Vetch, the rabbit from Golden Brook they had met when rescuing the hammer, Surestrike. It was unusual to see him out of the kitchens these days, but Podkin was too worried to think much about it.

"That's it," Dodge was saying. "There's nothing else to do this time. We have to leave. Get away from the forest completely."

"We still have some time," said Crom. "How fast do you

think they were going? It might be months before they reach us."

"We can't wait that long!" said Lady Enna. "What about our sick rabbits? What about my children? We must keep them safe!"

"We could counterattack," said Rill. "Blow up those machines with some of Mash's bang-dust. That would buy us time."

"There are still refugees coming in," said Mish. "Word is out about us now. We can't just vanish when we've worked so hard to give rabbits hope."

"Where would we go to, anyway?" said Paz. "Even if we find another warren on the other side of Grimheart, we'll have to run again if the Gorm really are going to mow the whole forest down."

A *warren on the other side of Grimheart.* That gave Podkin an idea. "What about Uncle Hennic?" he said. "He's the chieftain of Sparrowfast Warren."

Paz tutted. "I just *said*, there's no point running to another warren on the other side of the forest. Weren't you listening?"

"But he has a Gift, doesn't he?" Podkin continued. "I remember Father saying. Isn't it a bow?"

"A bow, yes, but—" his mother began, then was interrupted by Brigid chuckling.

"I was wondering when someone would remember

that," Brigid said. "I should have seen that it would be you, Podkin."

"Of course! A bow!" Paz kissed Podkin on the cheek. "We need a bow to use the three special Gormkiller arrows! We can escape from the Gorm *and* find a way to fight back!"

"But what about the refugees?" Mish said. "And Sparrowfast is a long march away. We still have sickly rabbits here." She looked over to the fireside where Podkin's Auntie Olwyn dozed, along with two other rabbits.

"What about sending an advance party?" Podkin didn't recognize the voice at first, then was surprised to see it was Vetch. "Some could go on ahead, and the rest could follow later, at their own pace."

"Would you be volunteering to go, by any chance?" said Crom. He had never trusted the ginger-furred rabbit much.

"I don't mind," said Vetch, fiddling with the golden thread on his embroidered cloak. "If I could be spared here. I do know the way, as my warren used to trade with them in the past. They breed the best messenger sparrows in the Five Realms."

"I'm not sure about this," Podkin's mother said. "My brother and I haven't spoken in years. We didn't part on very good terms . . ."

"Then perhaps you should follow on later," said Crom. "You can bring your sister, Olwyn. Sorrel can come with you, along with Surestrike. We can't leave any of the Gifts here, just in case. I will go ahead with Podkin and some others. We need to persuade Hennic to let us use his bow, and a family quarrel might get in the way."

"Good luck persuading him of anything," Lady Enna muttered, but nobody except Podkin heard her.

———◦∞◦———

By the next morning, the advance party was ready. It consisted of Podkin, Paz, Pook, Crom, Yarrow, Dodge, Rill, and Vetch, to lead the way. Tansy, the warrior from Applecross, brought the Gormkiller arrows. A second group — including Podkin's mother and aunt, along with Brigid and Sorrel to look after them — would follow at a slower pace in a few days. The rabbits Brigid had nursed back to health were still quite weak, some needing sticks to walk. And there was also an agreement that it was better for the Dark Hollow council to smooth things over with Chief Hennic before Lady Enna arrived on the scene.

Mish, Mash, and the scouts would stay behind until the very last moment, risking the Gorm's arrival in order to make sure any straggling refugees could find them. It was a very brave thing to do, and Podkin couldn't help wishing the dwarf rabbits were coming along with him, but they had absolutely insisted. There was no arguing with a dwarf rabbit once its mind was set.

The thought of the forest being eaten, Dark Hollow destroyed, another home lost . . . it was almost too much for Podkin. He stood with the rest of his group, pack on his back, resting a paw against the great oak doors of the warren. He didn't want to let go, imagining it being ground to sawdust by the Gorm's nightmarish machines. He might never see it again.

Paz finally had to pry his little hand away, whispering in his ear, "It'll be fine, Pod. We'll be back soon; you'll see. We'll find a way to stop the Gorm from destroying the forest."

Podkin wasn't sure, but he let himself be led across to where Crom was waiting. The big warrior put a gentle paw on his head. Podkin's mother was fussing over Pook, sniffing away tears and making Yarrow promise for the seven hundredth time that he would take care of him.

She came and cried over Podkin and Paz, too, rubbing noses, straightening cloaks, and making them swear they would be careful.

"We're only walking through the forest, Mother," Podkin said. "You'll be behind us as well. We'll see you in a few days."

"I know, I know. But . . ." She was led away by Auntie Olwyn, who blew the children a kiss farewell.

Brigid was next to say goodbye. She had a sad, pained look on her face. Podkin remembered it from the time she sent them off to Boneroot. It was never good news when someone who knew the future looked at you like that.

"What is it?" Podkin asked as she stooped down to hug him. "What's going to happen to us this time?"

"Nothing that doesn't need to, my dear," she said, not able to meet his eye. "Just trust in the Goddess, won't you? And look after each other. Like you've always done."

"It's something awful, isn't it?" Podkin said. "Can't you just tell us?"

Brigid shook her head. "Whatever I say might change the path. Whatever I don't say might change it too." She gave a deep sigh, ears drooping. "I'm so tired of this burden. Of always *knowing*. Be careful, Podkin. The forest has secrets. And so do those around you."

Podkin wanted to ask more, but their group was off. A cluster of rabbits from the warren pushed forward to shout goodbye, and Brigid was lost in the crowd. Crom took Podkin's hand and led him onward, and then they were walking away from Dark Hollow, into the forest, into whatever danger Brigid was trying to warn them of.

—∿—

They took one of the scout paths through the trees, following it until it met up with the main track south. The rutted road was where carts from Silverock Warren cut through the forest, bringing barrels of their famous mead to trade with the warrens of Gotland and Enderby.

Once they were on the track, their progress was quite fast. They broke for a quick lunch, then pressed on, hoping to be halfway there by nightfall. Podkin didn't fancy camping out in the middle of the forest with no burrow to hide in, but there weren't any warrens that deep inside Grimheart. Possibly because the trees were so thick, or maybe there was no space for farming. *Or it could be because of the Beast,* his mind added. *The legendary Beast of Grimheart that has terrified everyone.*

Crom had grown up in the forest and said he had never seen a beast. He even suggested that the old Dark Hollow rabbits had made up the legend to keep other rabbits away. If they had, they'd done a good job. Warrens all around told tales of the mysterious creature: a horned being, three times the size of a grown rabbit, who would eat you for breakfast if you wandered too far into the forest.

Tales to scare kittens, Podkin told himself. He had never believed a word of it before. But now he couldn't help looking at the deep woods around him as they walked. At the blackness between the trees, where it was cold and dark and hungry.

He hurried his pace to walk beside Paz, hoping for a chat to keep his imagination quiet.

"So," he said, "what's the problem between Mother and Uncle Hennic? I don't think we've ever met him, have we?"

"I think I did when I was very young," said Paz. "You probably weren't even born."

"Did they have an argument or something?" Podkin pressed on. "Or was it just because he took one look at you and decided to pretend we weren't related?"

Paz cuffed him on his good ear and scowled. "It was way before that, badger breath. You wouldn't understand, anyway. You're too young."

"Try me."

Paz sighed. "All right. If it'll keep you quiet. Mother told me about it back in Munbury, before ... you know, *before.*

"Apparently it was something to do with Father. Hennic and Mother grew up together at Sparrowfast. Their father, our grandfather Uthric, was chief. Mother was the eldest, like me, but Hennic was next in line. He knew it, too, and was always putting Mother down about it. How she would never be anything special and he was going to be chief. Mother said her father was just as bad, ignoring her most of the time and treating Hennic like a little prince.

"Anyway, it so happened that Chief Bodkin of Munbury (that's our grandfather on Father's side, in case you hadn't worked it out) thought Mother would make a perfect wife for his son. Munbury was a bigger warren than Sparrowfast, and it was a good match. It also meant Mother would be Lady Enna and become just as important — if not more so — as Uncle Hennic. Chief Uthric was suddenly very proud of Mother then, and it put Hennic's ears in a twist. He's done everything he can to avoid her since. The two of them *hate* each other."

Podkin thought of his sister and how he and she bickered most of the time. He'd never want them to end up hating each other, though. The idea of them not speaking, not always being together . . .

"I'm sorry I was rude about you, Paz," he said. "We won't ever fall out like that, will we?"

Paz looked down at her little brother and gave him a playful shove. "Not a chance, pipsqueak. We're together forever, you and I."

"Pook! Pook!" Their baby brother had been looking at them over the back of Yarrow's shoulder and suddenly thought he was being left out.

"And you, Pook," Podkin called to him. "You'll always be with us too."

—⁓—

It got dark very quickly in the depths of the forest. There were patches of sky above through which the moon shone down and the first stars were beginning to shine. It must have been early evening, but in between the trees, it was getting hard to see. They lit a lantern and carried on for a while longer but soon began to trip over roots and potholes. All except Crom, who lived his whole life in the dark and seemed to have a sixth sense about where to place his feet.

After Yarrow had stumbled for the tenth time, he gave a dramatic sigh and addressed the group. "For the sake of my poor toes and ankles, do you think we might be allowed to stop for the night? A meal and a slumber beneath the stars would be divine right about now."

Crom seemed about to argue, but with all the other rabbits beginning to drop their packs, he didn't have much choice. They found a clear spot beside the road and began to build a campfire.

"Soop! Soop!" Pook began shouting almost immediately. Vetch had a packful of cooking supplies and began chopping and preparing vegetables while Rill set up a tripod over the blossoming fire for the cooking pot. Pook sat close to the flames, watching everything with hungry eyes.

"No soup for you, Pook," said Paz, drawing him away. "Brigid has given us some special carrot cakes."

As Paz took the leaf-wrapped cakes from her backpack,

Podkin came and joined them, ear pricked at the mention of Brigid's name.

"Carrot cakes? Why just for us?"

"They have chamomile in them," said Paz. "For a good night's sleep and sweet dreams. She didn't want us to be scared, sleeping out in the forest."

Podkin wasn't sure—the soup was starting to smell quite delicious—but he also didn't want to turn down some of Brigid's delicious treats. The three of them set upon the cakes as soon as they were unwrapped, with Pook eating two whole ones by himself. By the time the soup was ready for the others, all three little rabbits were wrapped in their blankets, huddled by the fireside, with their eyes starting to close. It had been a long day.

A Knife in the Night

Podkin was having a nightmare about forest spiders crawling inside his cloak. *So much for sweet dreams,* he thought as he awoke, only to find a spider still there, legs rummaging at his tunic collar.

He screamed and sat bolt upright, scrabbling at his neck. The fire had died down but was bright enough to give the clearing a dim orange glow. The "spider" had left his throat now, and Podkin could see that it was actually a paw, one belonging to Vetch.

"What's wrong? What's happening?" Paz was awake now too, along with Pook, who had been curled up with her. They both stared over at Podkin, Paz's paw on the hilt of Ailfew.

"Vetch?" Podkin said. "What are you doing?" The

Golden Brook rabbit was hunched near him, firelight glinting on the colored threads of his exotic cloak. There was a look in his eyes that Podkin hadn't seen before: greedy, sly, dangerous. *None of the others woke up when I screamed,* Podkin realized. *What has Vetch done to them?*

"Get away from Podkin, Vetch," said Paz, beginning to raise Ailfew. But the ginger-furred rabbit was quicker. He drew his cook's knife and jumped at Podkin, seizing him by the ear and pressing the blade to Pod's neck.

"I don't think so," said Vetch. "Put the sickle down. And if I see you trying to do your magic, I'll cut your brother's throat."

Podkin could feel the edge of the knife. It was a thin, sharp line, already slicing his fur, lying hot against the pink skin underneath. Paz lowered Ailfew but shifted Pook up onto her chest, ready to leap up with him if she had to.

"What have you done to the others?" she asked, her voice shaking. Crom, Yarrow, and the rest were still huddled in their blankets, lifeless lumps in the firelight.

"They're asleep, I think." Vetch's eyes twitched to and fro, his ears flicking and jittering. "Or dead. Who knows? I stole a sleeping potion from your know-it-all witch friend, but I had no idea how much to use. She didn't see *that* coming, did she?"

Podkin felt like kicking himself. Crom had never

trusted Vetch, but Podkin had wanted to give him a chance. If only he'd listened. If only he hadn't been so worried about hurting the ginger rabbit's feelings. "What do you want, Vetch?" he managed to ask, despite the knife at his throat.

"It's obvious, isn't it?" Vetch said, sneering. "Your magic Gifts. All three of them. If you'd only eaten the soup, you'd be asleep too, and I could have taken them without any of this tiresome drama."

"But why?" Paz asked. "We took you in. We trusted you."

"Oh, yes." Vetch laughed. "Trusted me to work in the kitchens! Trusted me to be your pot-scrubbing slave! How very noble of you. Don't you have any idea who I am?"

"A sneaky traitor!" Podkin shouted. "We should have left you for the Gorm!"

"Shut up!" Vetch pushed the knife harder against Podkin's throat. He could feel a burning sting, and a trickle of blood ran down inside his tunic. "You jumped-up little weasel! I am the heir to Golden Brook Warren! In fact, as my father is probably dead himself, I am actually the chief. And you worthless bunch of rabble have had me peeling potatoes for you when you should have been groveling at my feet!"

"Calm down," said Paz, her eyes not leaving the blade at Podkin's throat. Pook was starting to whimper, and she clutched him tighter. "There's no need for shouting. Just tell us . . . Are you working for the Gorm? Is that why you want the Gifts?"

Vetch laughed again. A crazy, broken, high-pitched noise. "What do you think? Of course I'm working for them! And I'm going to give your Gifts to Scramashank himself. We've made a deal. It's a bargain you should have made yourselves, if you'd had any sense. Nobody can stop the Gorm. The world is theirs. Only the warrens that help them can hope to survive."

"But you've seen what they do," said Paz. "They're not going to spare you. They'll just take your warren, turn you into one of them."

"No, not Golden Brook," said Vetch. "Scramashank promised. He said he would spare it if we shared our riches with him and if we brought him one of the Gifts. I thought I might travel south to an ancient warren—offer to buy their Gift from them—when I fell in with Zarza and then you lot. And what should I find you had? Three of the Gifts! Three! And then you got the hammer, too! Imagine what the Gorm will give me for *this* prize."

"You're mad!" Paz shouted. "You can't trust them—they're monsters!"

Vetch gave his crazed laugh again. "You silly little country rabbit! You don't know anything about how the world works. You think they're monsters just because they want something different from what you do. Have you ever tried talking to them? Have you ever thought about making a deal?"

"Talk? They tried to kill us! Several times!"

Despite the knife at his throat, a horrible thought had occurred to Podkin. The Gorm were chopping down the forest — why hadn't they started farther east or west? How had they known to begin their attack directly north of Dark Hollow?

"Have you been talking to your masters, Vetch?" he managed to say. "Have you told them where we're hiding?"

Vetch took his eyes off Paz for a moment to give Podkin a glare. It was a look of pure disgust, as if Pod were a pile of weasel dung at the end of his knife blade. "Of course I have. I've told them where your poky little warren is, how many of you there are . . . even what you're planning to do with those three stupid arrows you've made."

"You two-faced ginger weasel!" Paz couldn't believe the depths this traitorous rabbit had sunk to. "How did you even get a message out? How didn't we know?"

"You think you're so clever, don't you?" Vetch pushed his knife harder against Podkin's neck, then pulled something from his own tunic with his other hand. Looking up, Podkin could see a golden locket on a fine chain. When Vetch popped it open, there was a small glass vial inside. A vial that contained a sliver of Gorm iron, writhing like a worm on a fishhook. "They gave me a piece of their god,"

Vetch said, grinning and cackling. "Hidden inside gold so that your stupid witch friend wouldn't sense it. I thought she would, you know, every time she came near me. But they were right. They're always right. Gold hides it, makes it quiet until it's needed. They said I can open the locket and talk to the iron and they will hear me, and when they have the Gifts . . . oh, how happy they will be!"

All the while Vetch was talking, Podkin was frantically thinking. At the mention of Gifts, he remembered his own. His blanket was too tangled about his body for him to reach Starclaw, but the moon brooch might work. He raised his head as high as he could and looked up through the trees, searching for a patch of sky. There was a glimpse, back where the road was, and sure enough, the moon could be seen. Would he be able to jump without hurting himself further on Vetch's knife blade? He didn't think so, but there wasn't any other way out.

"Enough talking now," Vetch said, sensing the little rabbits were playing for time. "Give me the Gifts, and I promise not to hurt you. You can stay here until your friends wake up and then do whatever you want. Run to Sparrowfast; run to Thrianta. I don't care."

"Bite my whiskers," Podkin said. He focused his will on the shadows cast by the campfire and *pushed*.

Blink.

There was a tilt in the world, and Podkin vanished

from Vetch's grip. He felt a sharp sting in his neck as he jumped; then he was out of his blankets, appearing in the shadows next to his sister and looking back at Vetch, who just stood there, stunned. A thick drop of blood ran down his cook's knife to plop on the forest floor.

"Get up, Paz!" Podkin shouted. "Run!"

His sister threw her blanket back toward Vetch, and then the three little rabbits were away, bursting out of the clearing, across the track, and into the forest, once more running for their lives.

Interlude

The bard pauses there, looking around at his audience, whom he expects to be sitting forward in their seats, breath held, eyes popping. The bonedancers haven't moved a whisker. Three hundred pairs of cold eyes stare back at him like glass beads in a set of very creepy statues.

Rue, however, has practically tied his ears in knots. He presses his hands together and mouths words at the bard: *Don't stop there! Don't stop!*

But the bard *has* stopped, for the moment, and is smacking his lips in a very exaggerated manner. Right about now is when he usually gets presented with a flagon of mead or a mug of ale. A cup of tea at the very least.

"Would you like something to drink?" Sythica asks, finally taking the hint.

"Oh, yes, please," says the bard. "If you would be so kind."

The Mother Superior twitches an ear at one of the initiates, who scurries off and comes back with a glass of water. The bard holds it up to the light and looks at it, an eyebrow raised in disappointment.

When it is clear he isn't going to get anything better, he takes a few gulps, then wipes his mouth with the back of his sleeve.

"I take it this is the part of the story that the Golden Brook rabbits objected to?" Sythica asks as the initiate takes the bard's glass away from him.

"Part of it, yes," says the bard. "Although it does get worse."

"And was this Vetch already the chieftain when you told the tale?"

"No. No, he wasn't," says the bard. His jaw is clenched, as if to say that he would have been doing something else to Vetch, should he have seen him, rather than telling stories. Something involving a big stick and improvised dental work.

"But obviously some rabbits descended from him," says Sythica, "to have taken it so personally."

"His great-nephew, I believe," says the bard. "The whole warren was living under the delusion that he was some kind of hero. 'Vetch the Valorous,' they called him."

"And you decided to set them straight."

"As I said to my apprentice just this morning," says the bard, "some stories are told to tell the truth. I thought they deserved to hear it."

"Of all the weapons known to rabbit," says Sythica, "the truth can be the deadliest. Is there much more of the tale to come?"

For one horrible moment, Rue thinks she might tell the bard to finish right there. He almost jumps from his bench to object, but the bard is smiling his showman's smile again.

"Quite a bit," he says, bowing. "Including a guest appearance by members of your wonderful order. Are you not enjoying it?"

Sythica blinks once or twice, but the eyes behind the bone-and-silver mask don't betray the slightest bit of emotion.

"Oh, yes," she says. "We are enjoying it immensely, aren't we, sisters?"

As one, the bonedancers nod, then resume their stone-like poses. *Could have fooled me*, thinks the bard, trying to remember a worse crowd. He finds he cannot, maybe because most other audiences haven't listened with the express purpose of deciding whether or not to kill him.

"In that case," he says, "I shall continue."

Rue untwists his ears and sits back, ready to enter the depths of Grimheart Forest again.

Beast

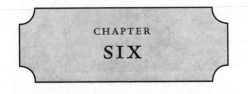

They ran though the dark forest, weaving between trees, paths forgotten.

Roots trapped their feet; branches whipped at their ears. Trunks of pine and spruce loomed out of nowhere. They bounced and crashed off them, stumbling in the dark, going deeper and deeper into the wild, knotted core of Grimheart Forest.

All the while they could hear, beneath the rattling and panting of their own breath, the snapping branches and rustling leaves behind them. Vetch was still coming: desperate, furious. He had no choice now but to kill them and take the Gifts. Podkin and Paz both knew it. It was life or death, and there was nobody around to help them.

They stopped for a few seconds to rest their bruised

legs and catch their breath. Pook was mewling and cling-ing tight to Paz's neck. Carrying him while running had made her back muscles burn like fire. Podkin had sprinted so fast, his head was spinning. His knees felt as weak as melted butter and . . . what was that *pitter-patter* noise he kept hearing? Had it started to rain?

"Podkin," Paz managed to speak in between gasps, "Podkin, you're *bleeding!*"

Bleeding what? Podkin thought, his mind feeling fuzzy. He put a hand to his tunic. He had been sweating so much that it was sticking to his skin.

Except it wasn't sweat.

He pulled his paw away and looked at it. *Black*, he thought. *Why am I covered in black paint?*

It smelled hot and coppery, like when Zarza was wounded by the spear. Just like that. *Exactly* like that. *Oh, dear*, Podkin thought. *It isn't paint after all.*

Just as Paz reached for him, Podkin's legs gave out and he stumbled to the mossy forest floor. The cut from Vetch's knife was much deeper than he'd first thought. He'd been bleeding all this time, leaving a red trail through the forest. *Maybe Crom can follow it when he comes to save me*, Podkin thought, although Crom wouldn't be waking up for hours yet (if at all). Pod's thoughts had become woozy and dream-like. The moss beneath him felt so soft and cozy, just right for a snooze . . .

"Podkin, wake up!" Paz whispered fiercely, pulling at his ear. She set Pook—who instantly started to wail when he saw the blood—next to Podkin and rummaged in her pack for her healing things. The sound of crashing branches was getting louder. She knew Vetch was coming closer . . . would be on them at any second.

"Pook! Be quiet!" she hissed, pulling out a wad of bandages and pressing them to the wound on Podkin's throat. It was too dark to see how bad it was, and she prayed to the Goddess that the sharp cook's knife hadn't nicked the jugular vein.

"Got . . . you . . ." a voice came from behind them. A breathless, wheezy, sly voice, full of sour smugness, despite the panting. Vetch had followed the trail of blood and found them.

"Just let me bind his throat," Paz said. "You can have the Gifts in a minute. Just let me help my brother."

"No," said Vetch. "No more tricks. It doesn't matter now, anyway."

It *doesn't matter because he's going to kill us*, Podkin thought. From where he lay, he could see past his sister to where Vetch was emerging from the trees, knife raised. Perhaps it was the loss of blood, but Podkin felt strangely calm about it. I'm going to see Father again, he thought. Dying isn't so bad after all.

As Paz fumbled at his throat with the bandages, Podkin watched Vetch draw nearer. He really was feeling quite dizzy now and had even started to imagine he was seeing things. Things moving among the trees. Was the forest coming alive? Was the darkness forming shapes and coming out to greet them?

One particularly large blob of shadow was moving *very* close. It slipped from tree to tree until it reached a small patch of moonlight in between Vetch and his prey. Podkin stared as it emerged from the gloom, a paw at first, then a leg, a snout, eyes . . .

A rumbling, snarling sound came from the living shadow. It stopped Vetch in his tracks, and Podkin realized the thing wasn't just a figment of his imagination. It was something *real* and very, very solid.

Both Paz and Vetch fell silent and turned to face the source of the growling. Everyone froze, staring as the thing took another step, letting the moonlight flow over it, revealing itself in all its awesome glory.

A *wolf,* Podkin thought. *But it doesn't look like any wolf I've ever seen.* That amounted to a few pictures on tapestries and carvings, and a lone gray wolf they had spotted in the woods near Redwater Warren one summer. *That* wolf had been enough to terrify them, but it was just a little cub compared to this thing.

This wolf's back was as tall as a fully grown rabbit, with thick dusky fur that was dappled with moon shadow. Muscles bunched at its shoulders and neck. Its head hung low, ready to attack. It had a long nose, amber eyes that glowed from within, and a mouth of such teeth . . .

"Fangs," Podkin whispered. Paz was too frozen with fear to agree. The giant wolf had canine teeth that stretched down past either side of its lower jaw, eight inches long at least. Teeth curved like deadly white sabers. This was no common gray or timber wolf from the forest's edge. This was a whole different breed. Some timeless, ancient species of creature that had lived in the heart of the forest, hidden away from the rabbit world. A true creature of the woods: a child of Hern the Hunter himself.

The four rabbits watched as the wolf took another step toward them. None of them could have moved a muscle, even if they wanted to.

They stared as the beast sniffed the air in the children's direction, then in Vetch's. It lowered its nose to the ground, its eyes watching them all the time. A splatter of Podkin's blood was there, glinting in the moonlight. With saber teeth brushing the moss, the wolf put out a long pink tongue and lapped it up.

I *hope* I *taste really horrible*, Podkin thought. I *hope it doesn't want any more.*

The wolf raised its head again and looked from Vetch to the children, then from the children to Vetch. It was quite obvious that the thing was making up its mind whom to eat first.

Vetch must have had the same idea. Suddenly he could move again, and he let out a squeak and turned to run back the way he had come. *Probably hoping the wolf chooses us first,* Podkin thought. *A nice, easy meal that can't run very far.*

But the wolf had other ideas. With a glance that said, *You're dessert. I'll get to you later,* it loped off after Vetch, sliding among the trees like a pike stalking minnows through pond reeds.

Podkin and Paz watched it go, then both let out the breath that had been frozen in their chests.

"Do you think you can stand?" Paz asked. "We need to get out of here before that . . . *thing* . . . comes back."

"Doggy!" Pook cooed, looking back to where the creature had disappeared.

"Wolf, Pook," Podkin started to say, but his voice was very shaky. Paz helped him to his feet, and they started to stagger in the opposite direction from where Vetch and the wolf had gone.

Leaning on his sister, Podkin hobbled along as best he could. They had no idea where they were going. They just knew they had to keep moving, hoping that somehow they could put enough distance between them and the wolf that it would not find them when it returned for its second course.

Paz was clutching Pook with one arm and propping up the weakened Podkin with the other. *Funny,* thought Pod (although there was nothing amusing about it), *this is how it all started: us running away, Paz holding me up because I couldn't walk.*

In his fuddled mind, the event became mixed up with ancient memories of rabbitkind being chased and devoured by anything with teeth.

"Everything always wants to eat us, Paz," he said, slurring the words.

"I know," replied his sister through gritted teeth.

—◁◇▷—

Paz's arms soon started to burn and weaken, her shoulder joints feeling as if they were about to pop, but still she struggled on.

This deep in the forest, there were gigantic trees with low branches interlacing and hanging down to snag and tear ears and fur. The forest floor was a thick sponge of dead leaves and pine needles. Only a thin haze of moonlight managed to filter down from the sky above, leaving Paz to squint and weave her way through the shadows.

"Podkin," she said at one point, thinking she couldn't go on much farther, "can't you use the brooch? Jump us through the shadows?"

"Not enough sky," Podkin muttered. "And I'm too weak." Jumping with the brooch used his energy, and he had precious little left.

Paz somehow found the strength to go farther. There seemed to be a path in front of them, an opening at least, although she could have sworn it wasn't there a moment ago.

"What do you think has happened to Vetch?" Podkin whispered.

"I don't know, Pod," Paz said. "I haven't heard any screams. I expect he *would* have screamed when the wolf got him. Wouldn't he?"

As if in answer, there came a snapping of branches from their left. The pine branches rustled. Something was following them through the trees.

"Maybe that's him," Podkin said. His hand pawed at the dagger on his belt.

"Him or the wolf," said Paz, tears in her eyes. "Oh, Podkin, I can't carry you anymore. I'm sorry."

She set her two brothers down and knelt beside them, arms numb, pulling Ailfew from her belt. She raised it in front of her, trying to center herself, reaching out for the roots and plants all around. If she could summon them, she could make some kind of a cage around the three of them. Would that be enough to hold off what was in the trees? Probably not, but what else was there to do?

Podkin watched his sister, her terrified face going in and out of focus. He managed to struggle to a sitting position and pulled Starclaw from his belt. There was no strength left in his little arms, but he might be able to aim the blade. It would cut through anything, including the flesh and bone of a giant wolf.

The rustling in the branches grew louder. They could hear a quiet snuffling and the crunch of heavy paws on the forest floor. In the dark between the trees, two points of light appeared, growing closer and closer.

"Doggy?" said Pook, holding out a chubby paw.

The wolf stepped onto the pathway, emerging into the moonlight once more. Its curved fangs glowed white, framing its mouth. Pook would be gone in one bite. Those amber eyes watched them with the patient calm of a hunter, taking in the knife and sickle, calculating the best angle of attack—

"H*ult!*"

A voice came from somewhere on the path ahead. A deep, rumbling voice that sounded like the forest itself talking.

The wolf looked up at once, ears pricked, nose twitching. Recognizing the scent, it lowered its mighty head and stepped silently back into the shadows.

The little rabbits looked around, trying to catch a glimpse of who had saved them. The branches on the path ahead parted, and a figure stepped out. Just a silhouette against the moonlight, but Podkin could see he was impossibly tall and broad, bigger than any rabbit he had ever seen. A pair of stag's horns stretched up and out from his head. There was only one being with horns like that. Now Podkin was sure he was dreaming.

"Hern," he whispered. "Hern the Hunter."

"No, Pod," Paz whispered back. "That's not a god. Crom was wrong. It *is* real. The Beast. The Beast of Grimheart."

More Beasts

The little rabbits all held their breath as the horned creature stepped closer. Branches cracked as it moved toward them, setting its heavy feet down on the path with solid thumps.

They could see that it held a staff as thick as a young tree, and that it had rough, shaggy hair covering its body. Rabbit or wild animal: Which was it? Would it rip them apart now, or tie them up and drag them off to its larder?

It took another step, then began to crouch. Podkin could hear the creature sniffing, like a wolf or bear. Paz raised the sickle, her paws shaking, as if it would do any good against this *thing*. Pod's weak hand raised Starclaw. He felt it judder as it sensed his fear, even though he had no strength left to use it.

The creature gave a hoot—a rumbling sound that made Podkin's whiskers tremble. Slowly, gently, it put down its staff, then moved its massive paw to its own chest. There was a fumbling, rustling noise. Was it scratching fleas? Did it have some horrible weapon hidden in its fur? Podkin and Paz blinked, fearing the worst but unable to do anything about it. Even Pook was silent for once.

Then—a bloom of light. Blue light. It came from the creature's hand, illuminating its face, the three little rabbits, and the pine branches hanging low over their heads.

Podkin stared. This wasn't a god or, as Paz said, a beast. It was just a rabbit, although a giant one—bigger even than those he had seen in Boneroot—but nothing from a myth or monster story at all.

In the blue glow he could see that the horns were part of a headdress, bound in place with twisted vines and decorated with pieces of carved bone. His face—and it had to be a he, judging by the long, braided beard—had a thick brow, broad nose, and deep-set brown eyes. The shaggy fur was a cloak of coarse wolfskin, complete with claws and snout, draped over the rabbit's shoulders. Underneath, he wore clothes of stitched leather and fur, with crossed straps over his chest. These were covered with more carved bones, amulets, strings of wooden beads, animal skulls, polished stones, flint knives, arrowheads, pockets, flasks, and pouches. One of these was now in his hand. It was filled with glowing blue moss of a type Podkin had never seen before.

"Wund?" the rabbit said. His voice was deep but gentle. Like a breeze blowing through a hollow oak tree. Podkin couldn't understand the language, but he looked into his eyes and saw only kindness and concern there. With a relief that made him feel dizzy again, he realized they were safe.

"Wund?" the rabbit said again. He pointed at Podkin's throat. In the light, the blood could clearly be seen, spattered all over his cloak and tunic.

"Yes," said Paz, also sensing the stranger meant them no harm. "He's cut his neck. Look."

She carefully moved the bandages she had wadded in place there. Podkin felt the blood start to flow again and, with it, another wash of weakness.

The giant rabbit made a tutting sound and reached for more of his pouches. His thick fingers were surprisingly nimble, and they pulled out a selection of wooden pots, each one beautifully carved with picture-like runes. Arranging them on the ground, the rabbit popped off the lids and went to work. He gave Podkin a strip of bark to chew, which tasted bitter but instantly started to numb first his mouth, then the rest of his body. He used a pinch of spongy moss from another tub to clean the wound, and then scooped out some gooey cream from a third, which he smeared over Podkin's cut. It felt cool and soothing, and Podkin imagined it gumming up the gash, sealing his blood inside.

Finally, the stranger took a flask from his belt, popped out the stopper, and held it to Podkin's mouth. The little rabbit drank deeply and tasted the purest, freshest water that was somehow full of every scent and flavor of the forest itself. It washed away all his dizziness and calmed his frazzled nerves. The escape from Vetch, the chase through the forest, the wolf . . . it just seemed like a bad dream he'd woken from.

Podkin made a contented sound, and then the big rabbit offered the flask to Paz. She had been watching his every move, trying to identify the herbs and plants he was using, but eagerly took the bottle and had a swallow or two before Pook snatched it from her paws and started trying to guzzle the whole thing. The giant rabbit laughed, a rumble that sounded like a landslide of boulders, and gently pulled it from the baby rabbit's grip.

He started to put away his things before pulling out some of the glowing moss and wrapping it about the top of his staff. It lit the forest around them like a lantern.

"*Kommen yon, du Grimwode,*" he said, standing and pointing deeper into the forest. He made beckoning motions with the staff, inviting them to follow.

"You want us to come with you?" Paz asked. She looked

back the way they had come, although there was nothing to be seen but twisted tree trunks and darkness. "We can't come. Our friends are back there . . ."

"*Kommen yon*," said the rabbit, gesturing again.

"Crom," Podkin tried to say, but his numb mouth made it sound like more of a gurgle.

"Yes, Crom," said Paz. "Crom and the others. We can't leave them. There's Vetch, and the wolf, and we don't know if they'll wake up . . ."

"*Kommen yon*." This time it was more of a statement. The giant rabbit reached down and scooped up Podkin as if he were a rag doll. In fact, that was pretty much what he felt like. He couldn't have resisted if he tried. Pook scrambled up the giant's arm too, leaving Paz with no choice but to follow.

"We really shouldn't," she tried to object, but what else could be done? If the giant left them, the wolf might return. Even if it didn't, it would be impossible to find their way back to the camp in the dark. Or even in the daytime, assuming they could survive on their own until then. They would have to go with this strange rabbit, find out what he wanted, and then try to return to the others somehow, when it was safe.

Podkin would probably have agreed, but he was fast asleep by then, being rocked back and forth like a kitten in its cradle as the giant rabbit strode through the forest, cupping him and Pook in the crook of his arm.

—⁓—

All through the rest of the night, the rabbit walked, with Paz trotting along beside him. Every time she stumbled, or stopped to catch her breath, the giant rabbit gave her a drink from the flask and she felt instantly refreshed, as if she had just jumped out of bed after a good night's sleep.

They marched and marched, deeper into the forest than Paz could have imagined, every step taking them farther away from their friends. Despite his enormous size, the giant made almost no noise as he moved. The branches and roots seemed to part before him, closing up again to leave no trace of his passing. Paz looked at the ground more than once to see if they were leaving tracks that Crom and Yarrow might be able to follow, but there were none. This creature was like a part of the forest itself, she realized. It cloaked him and hid him as if he were some kind of living, moving tree.

Every now and then, there was a rustle in the woods around them. Paz thought of that colossal wolf. Could it be following them? Maybe there were others . . . a whole pack?

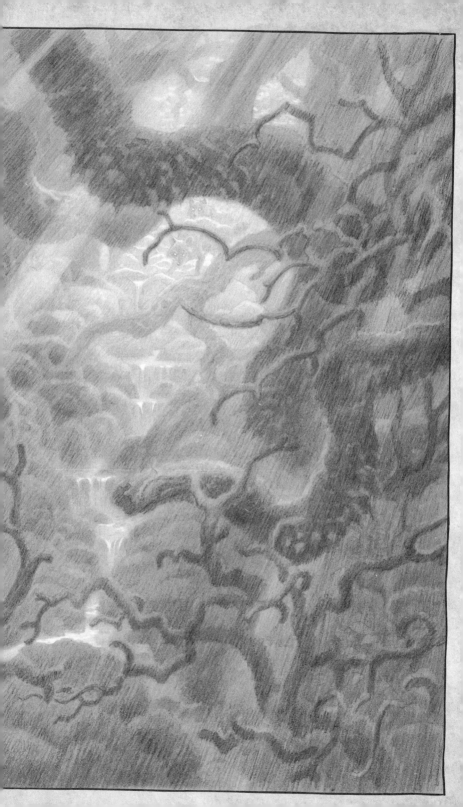

But with the giant rabbit beside her, Paz somehow knew there was nothing to fear. He showed no alarm, no matter how close the noises came. And even if the wolf did attack, the stranger would probably make short work of it. The wolfskin on his back was proof of that.

After they had been walking for Goddess knew how long, dawn started to break around them. Birdsong came first, followed by a gradual lightening of the shadows. From his cozy perch in the giant rabbit's arms, Podkin began to stir and look about. He gave Paz a weak smile, and the pair of them watched the forest begin to change as they moved deeper and deeper into its heart.

The first thing they noticed was the trees, which grew steadily thicker and taller, each bigger than the last, until the rabbits were walking among enormous, towering trunks with roots higher than Paz's head. Oaks, cedars, and elms, each one must have been older than all the trees around Dark Hollow put together. Their great size meant lots of space in between them on the forest floor, with swooping branches leaning down to make green-lit canopies. Twining patterns of dawn light danced over the soft, spongy earth.

Thick moss was everywhere, wrapping the roots and climbing up the trunks. It reminded Podkin of snow, shrouding everything and softening it into lumps and mounds. The overhanging branches were also cloaked in lichen, which hung down between the leaves like shaggy locks of green, blue, and white hair. It flecked the enormous trunks of the trees as if a painter had gone wild with a thousand brushes.

The air was full of glistening specks. Floating seeds, insects, motes of this and that. Everything moved lazily, as if the moments were passing slower here. The whole place felt ancient — older than time — but so packed with *life*. More than any other woods or forest Podkin had been in. He breathed deeply of the cool, pure scent: smelling the sap, the leaves, the drifts of humus on the floor. It refreshed him, filled him with peace after the terrifying events of the night before.

"It's so *old* here, Paz," he whispered, not wanting to disturb the slow hum of living, growing things around them.

His sister nodded. "I knew Grimheart was ancient, but I never imagined anything like *this*," she replied.

"*Yar bist du Grimwode*," said the giant rabbit, the first sound he'd made since picking Podkin up. He pointed straight ahead to where the trunks of the thickest trees yet stood, wide enough to fit whole warrens inside. It was hard to imagine that something living could be so big. The giant pointed and spoke again. "*Hern's Holt*."

It seemed as though they had arrived at their destination.

The enormous trees had grown in a circle. Their lowest branches were all at least fifty feet off the ground, creating a wide-open space in between the tree trunks. Looking up through the clouds of greenery, Podkin could see a circle of blue sky lighting the clearing with a hazy yellow glow.

The ground in between was vivid green, every inch covered in tides of moss. A small stream trickled through the middle, gathering in a pool where the shadows of large fish swam in lazy circles. There were lumps and bumps scattered all around the clearing. Objects under the mossy covering, like a giant version of toy wooden blocks beneath a carpet. Some were quite large; some were wrapped in roots or ivy. All were strangely formed: angles and lines clashed with the gentle natural shapes around them.

It took Podkin a while to realize they were ruins. Leftover stone structures from the time of the Ancients, like the pillars of Boneroot or the stone tomb at Applecross. One in particular was very large. It looked like some kind of tower with the roof missing. There were four walls, each with a circular gap at the top, where something important had once sat. Windows, maybe? Sculptures or icons? Did the Ancients have gods like the rabbits did? There was no way of knowing, and Podkin was filled with the same mixture of curiosity and sadness that he felt whenever he came across evidence of that lost, forgotten world. It was gone forever now. Almost swallowed completely by time and the growth of the forest around it.

Pulling his eyes away from the mossy tower, Podkin noticed the mouth of a large tunnel at its base. A thick curtain of ivy hung down, almost hiding it, but something was moving there. Could that be the entrance to the giant rabbit's burrow?

As if in answer, the ivy parted, and another huge rabbit emerged. Pook gave a squeal of excitement, but both Podkin and Paz tensed. This was when they would find out whether the new rabbits were truly friendly, or if the young rabbits had just been harvested for dinner.

The new rabbit walked up from the tunnel into the clearing and waved. It called out something in a mixture of hoots, clicks, and barks, which their rescuer replied to. It was nothing like the language they had heard him use before. It sounded like a blend of all the different sounds of the forest: birdcalls, fox yaps, and the creaking of trees mixed together.

Hopping over the stream, they made for the burrow. The two giant rabbits reached out to clasp arms, and the new one blinked in surprise when it saw Podkin, Paz, and

Pook. It bent down to examine them more closely and rumbled out a laugh when Pook reached up to tweak its nose.

This one was dressed differently from the one who had saved them. Instead of fur, its cloak was made of leaves of all shapes, sizes, and colors. It had horns on either side of its head too, but when Podkin looked closely, he could see they were made of branches rather than antlers. It had the same broad nose and heavy brow, and those deep, kindly brown eyes, but this one seemed older than the other. It was a little hunched and leaned more on the thick wooden staff it carried. It had long eyelashes and a softer, higher voice, making Podkin think it was female.

The two giants spoke for a few moments in their sing-song forest language, then turned to head down the tunnel into their warren. Paz hung back a second, looking up at Podkin and Pook, both clutched in the fur-clad rabbit's arms. Even though going down beneath the ground didn't seem like the best of ideas (no escape without hard digging; nowhere to run to), she didn't have a choice. With a silent prayer to the Goddess, she hurried after them.

———

The tunnel sloped downward quite steeply. It was just bare earth, nothing like the tiled and decorated entrances of other rabbit warrens. Clay oil lamps and candles had been placed in hollowed alcoves here and there, and every now and then, there was a glimpse of a gigantic root, poking out of the mud wall.

Down, down they went, until they came to a set of doors standing wide open. *No guards or sentries*, Podkin thought. *But then, who knew all this was hidden here? Has any rabbit ever even been this far into the forest?*

They stepped through the doors, and Podkin and Paz both gasped.

They had emerged into a wide, almost circular chamber. In an instant it was clear that the whole place was another part of the Ancients' ruins above. The walls were made of carved stone, cracked and worn by time. Overhead was a ceiling of arches, and the floor was tiled in patterns, with a large eight-pointed star in the center.

Roots had broken through all over but were trained and tended so that they flowed alongside the stonework, helping to support it. There were even one or two statues remaining. These must have been of the Ancients themselves. They were so old, it was difficult to make them out, but Podkin could recognize the tall earless beings he had seen carved in the tomb on Ancients' Island, with their long, spidery fingers, small eyes, and funny-shaped noses.

Arched doorways led off in different directions. The

giants headed through one of them and down a corridor into a broad chamber.

This room had walls of wood panels, leading up to a row of stone-carved windows that had once looked out on some long-forgotten view. The ceiling was now a mat of roots, which had poured in through every available gap. The whole scene was lit by clumps of that glowing blue moss, which grew in luminous sprawls all over the broken woodwork, making the whole place seem odd and alien.

. . . As did its inhabitants: more giant rabbits — six or seven at least — all wearing horns and cloaks of different kinds. They were gathered in small groups, talking or making things. When the rabbit carrying Podkin and Pook entered, the others stopped and came over to look at the tiny newcomers. Podkin clutched Pook and made himself as small as possible. Paz tried to hide behind the giant rabbit's fur cloak.

From among the crowd of new giants, one stepped forward and peered at Podkin. This one, a female, had a patchwork cloak and the enormous antlers of some unknown breed of deer or elk on her head. She spoke in hoots and whistles, to which the wolf-furred rabbit replied. There was much pointing and miming, and Podkin couldn't help but wonder if they were discussing which spices went best with small rabbit, and what the cooking times might be.

Finally, the elk-horned one crouched low, bringing herself to eye level with Podkin and Pook.

"*Spakk Gott?*" she asked. When Pod and Pook just blinked back, she tried again. "Speak Lanic?"

"Speak?" Podkin said. "Umm . . . yes?"

"She's asking what language we speak, ferret brain!" Paz hissed at him from where she was hiding. "Tell her we speak Lanic. Tell her we understand!"

"Speak Lanic," the rabbit said again, this time a statement. "Good. I speak it too. I am Mo Grim. I am chief here. Welcome to Hern's Holt. Welcome to the Grimwode."

A wash of relief spread over Podkin as he realized there was a chance of talking sense to these rabbits. They would be able to find out where they were and what the giants wanted with them. They (probably) weren't going to be gobbled up like kittens in a fairy tale.

"Ask her what the Grimwode is," said Paz, thinking the same thing. "Ask her how we get home!"

The big rabbit laughed and put out a paw to Paz. "Come," she said. "Come sit with us, and we talk."

The giant rabbits formed a circle, and Podkin, Paz, and Pook were gently shepherded to the center. Their hosts went about fetching food and drink, while one approached Podkin and, with gestures of its hands, got him to show his neck wound. There was some hooting and clicking in their language, and more pots of cream and herbs were brought. As Chief Mo Grim began to speak, Podkin was gently cared for.

"We welcome you," she said again. "Not many rabbits come here. None since Shade. Many, many years ago. He taught some of us your words, your languages. Gott from Gotland and Lanic, the common tongue."

"Shade the Cursed!" Paz whispered to Podkin. He had been the chieftain of Dark Hollow generations ago. It was he who had buried Moonfyre, the brooch that Podkin now wore, before leaving his warren Giftless and doomed as punishment for not respecting the forest. The mystery of where he had gone was now solved.

"We found him lost in Grimheart. He lived with us until his death, and his knowledge is passed on."

"Who are you?" Paz asked. "What is this place?"

"The Grimwode," said Mo Grim, smiling. "This is the oldest part, the heart of the forest. The Ancients planted it themselves, even as their world was being eaten by Gormalech. Its roots are deep, and protected from that evil thing. The Ancients left Hern here to keep it safe."

Mo Grim ran a paw across the floor she sat on, protective, affectionate.

"Once, Gormalech covered all land and sea with its poison metal body, but not the Grimwode. The trees still grew; the forest was still green. When the goddesses returned and sent Gormalech under the ground, the Grimwode gave birth to the rest of the forest. All life came from here."

"Have you been here since then?" Podkin asked. The rabbit who was tending him had finished now. The cut on his neck didn't hurt as much; in fact, he could barely feel anything except a lovely, relaxing tingling all over.

Mo Grim laughed. "No, we are not that old! Our distant grandmothers and grandfathers found this place once the forest had grown all around. Hern led them here and made them his Wardens. Since then we have guarded the forest and cared for it. One Warden for each part."

"Part of what?" asked Paz.

"The forest," said Mo Grim. She began to point at the other rabbits to introduce them. "Rake is the one who found you. He tends the wolves and bears. Vendra met you at the door. Hers are the plants. There is Bole, tree Warden. That one is Chitna of the insects, and Vian of the birds. Cob there wards the spiders, and Litherus the reptiles. The little one is Pocka. He is only a baby, but he will grow to care for the mushrooms and toadstools."

The last rabbit she had pointed to was already nearly the size of Paz but was sitting at the edge of the circle, playing with some carved wooden dolls and smiling shyly at Pook. *All of this*, thought Podkin, *hidden away since time began. The secret realm of the forest god.*

"Is Hern here?" Podkin asked, looking around the

chamber. If a god suddenly stepped into the room, he probably wouldn't be that surprised, the way this day was going.

"Hern is everywhere," said Mo Grim. "He *is* the Grimwode, and the forest of Grimheart. Everything in it belongs to him."

"Hmm," said Paz, ears twitching in thought. "Brigid told us that the goddesses found the world and decided to trick it from Gormalech. But you're saying Hern was here all along?"

"Yes," said Mo Grim. "He was here through all the many centuries of Gormalech's rage. Safe within the Grimwode's protection. The goddesses didn't just find this place. They once *lived* here too, in the time of the Ancients, before they all had to flee. Hern called them back from the stars when the time was right, when the power of Gormalech had ebbed a little with age. And when they had beaten the evil one belowground, Hern took them to the secret tomb to claim the magic force the Ancients had left for them. Only we forest Wardens know this part of the tale. It was told to us by Hern himself."

"A secret tomb?" said Podkin. "Was it on an island?"

"Yes," said Mo Grim. "Hidden deep underneath."

"I bet that's where we found the hammer, Pod," said Paz. "I knew that place had been built to hold something special."

"That hammer was made from the magic force," Mo Grim said. "And the other Gifts. The goddesses took the force and crafted it for rabbits to wield. But you know this already. Rake says you have some of the Gifts yourselves."

At mention of this, both Podkin and Paz moved their paws to protect their treasures. Not that they would be able to stop even one of the giant rabbits from taking them.

"Do not worry," said Mo Grim, chuckling again. "Your Gifts are safe. We have old stories that told us you would be coming here one day."

"Us? Coming here?" Podkin looked around, wondering how a tiny thing like him could have anything to do with such an ancient, marvelous place.

"Yes. The Gift-Bearers," said Mo Grim, drawing nods and bows from the other Wardens. "The stories say you will come when the forest needs you. That we must take you to Oakhenge."

"Take us there for what?" Podkin asked, hoping it wouldn't have anything to do with the words "sacrifice" or "offering."

"To claim the Gift of Hern's Holt," said Mo Grim. "You will need it for the war."

"War?" Podkin and Paz said together, loudly enough to make Pook squeak. But food had been prepared, and the Wardens began to dish out bowls of mushroom stew and slabs of bread the size of Podkin's head.

Podkin and Paz realized they were ravenously hungry as they tucked in. All their questions would have to wait. As if in answer, Mo Grim smiled and nodded at them, speaking around a mouthful of food.

"Tomorrow," she said. "We will take you there tomorrow."

Blodcrun

After eating, even though it could only have been around midday, Podkin and Paz both fell into a deep, exhausted sleep.

The Warden rabbits left them snoring, quietly going about their jobs as before. Pook amused himself by playing with Pocka. The two shared toys and laughed and giggled together as Pook climbed onto Pocka's head and played peekaboo behind the enormous baby's ears.

At some point in the evening, Podkin woke and watched them, marveling at how two little rabbits could get along so well without any common language to help them. Or rather, they had their own language that never had to be learned: laughs and smiles and gestures that told each other simple things like "I am happy," "That was funny," and "You're my friend."

How easy it must be to be a baby, Podkin thought, envying his little brother for the first time. Even though Pod was just a few years older, his life had already become more complicated and difficult than he could ever have imagined.

Paz woke too, soon after, and the Wardens began preparing for another meal. They lifted stone slabs from the center of the chamber to expose a large fire pit, in which they quickly built a crackling blaze, complete with a tripod that held a pot big enough for Podkin to have taken a bath in. This was filled with mushrooms, herbs, nuts, seeds, and wild garlic and was soon bubbling away, releasing a delicious smell.

When ready, the stew was dished into bowls, and the Wardens all came to sit around the fire. Podkin and Paz had difficulty holding their soup bowls, they were so big. Pook just reached both paws into his bowl and started shoveling the stew into his mouth. It was spicy and earthy but delicious.

Podkin had ended up sitting next to Cob, the spider Warden, and at one point noticed that his cloak of carefully layered webs was moving. Looking closer, he spotted spiders of every size, silently scuttling about within. With a squeak, he edged away as quickly as he could (without being rude) and bumped into Paz, who was edging the other way. She had sat next to Chitna, and had herself just noticed the living beetles in *that* Warden's cloak. They shared a look of quiet horror and sat very still until dinner ended.

As soon as everyone had finished eating, the Wardens rose and began cleaning up. Podkin had a barrage of questions ready, but Mo Grim just looked at him and smiled. "Tomorrow," was all she said.

One by one, the Wardens left the chamber, off to their own burrows and beds elsewhere in the warren. Chitna picked up Pocka and cradled him so tenderly, it was obvious she was his mother. Pook began to raise a paw to wave, but that was too much effort for the little rabbit. He collapsed onto Paz's lap and fell into a deep sleep.

The last Warden to go (Podkin thought it might be Bole, the tree Warden, judging by his wooden armor and cloak of bark strips) left them a pile of blankets. Podkin and Paz arranged them into nests by the dwindling fireside and snuggled down, looking up to the blue-lit ceiling of intertwined roots above.

"What do you make of all this?" Podkin asked his sister. "These ruins?"

"Everything. The Wardens, the Grimwode, what Mo said..." Podkin waved his paws in the air, trying to express himself. "Everything."

Paz thought a moment. "Well, they haven't tried to take the Gifts from us, even though they easily could have. So I guess we can trust them. We'll let them take us to this oak place tomorrow and then see if we can get them to send us home. I'm guessing they know their way around the forest much better than we do."

"Mo said it was another Gift. Do you really think it is?"

"I guess," said Paz. She yawned.

"It would be good if it was. Although I don't like the sound of this war."

"We're already at war, silly," said Paz. "What do you think's happening between us and the Gorm?"

"Is that a war?" Podkin scratched the stump of his missing ear. "I thought wars were all big battles with armies and things."

"Be careful what you wish for," said Paz, yawning again. "Can we go to sleep now?"

"Just a few more questions," said Podkin, ignoring his sister's sigh. "I've been thinking about the Goddess and everything that's happened."

"Yes?"

"Well, do you think she really planned all this? I mean, the Wardens expected us to arrive, and Brigid seems to know the exact second I'm about to burp, even. Has it all been put in place, waiting for us to come along?"

"I have no idea, Pod." Paz watched sparks from the fire drift up to the twining roots overhead. "Maybe it has. Maybe the Goddess just had a plan in case Gormalech broke the Balance, and we happen to have stumbled into it. Who knows why anything happens?"

Podkin pondered that for a moment. It was a very big thought to tackle. He heard Paz's breathing beginning to deepen, but he had something else to say.

"Paz?"

"Mmmm? What?"

"Have you noticed something about the Wardens' chief?"

"She's very big?"

"No. She's a woman."

"Yes, Podkin. I had noticed that."

"And this tribe must have been around for a very long time."

"Ages, I expect."

"So that means that female rabbits must have been chieftains once upon a time. In Hern's Holt, but maybe everywhere else. That rule you hate so much ... about how only men can become chief ... perhaps it's just been made up?"

"I had thought of that," said Paz. "Not that it'll do any good."

"I think it will," said Podkin. He knew what his sister

wanted more than anything. He also knew that he was standing in the way of it. "I think we should tell the others, when we find them again. I think we should talk about it in the council and get them to say that you should be the chief of Munbury Warren. If we ever get back there, of course."

"But . . ." Paz sat up now, her eyes glinting at Podkin in the last sparks of the fire. "But don't you want to be chief? Everyone's always known it was going to be you."

Podkin shrugged and snuggled down into his blankets. "I don't mind. I don't think I'd be a very good chief, anyway. It's hard enough being on the war council—I'm always worried I'll say the wrong thing, or make a silly mistake."

"We all are, Podkin," said Paz. "That's how everyone in charge feels. That's how Father must have felt the whole time."

Father. Podkin hadn't thought of him for a while, what with all the fleeing for his life and everything. He felt a sudden pang of guilt and tried to picture him there, sitting by the fireside, looking down on his children. Podkin knew his father would be happy to see Paz get her dream, and he would too, he realized.

He smiled. "Good night, Chief Paz," he said, and pulled the blankets over his head, leaving his sister—suddenly wide awake—to stare at the embers and wonder.

Even though they had just slept through most of the day, the three little rabbits had a deep, restful night. They were woken by the bustling of the Wardens around them: relighting the cookfire and preparing breakfast.

"Good morning," said Mo Grim. "Today we go to Oakhenge." She handed them each a slab of coarse dark bread. Vian, with her cloak of feathers, was by the fireside, cooking a pan of scrambled eggs. "But first, Vendra wishes to check your wound."

The elderly Warden with her leaf cloak knelt down by Podkin and carefully removed his bandage. Paz craned her neck to see and was surprised to find that the cut had completely healed. There was nothing but a small line in Podkin's fur to show it was ever there.

"This place is very special," said Mo, smiling at Paz's expression. "It heals and restores rabbits. And those who stay here have very long lives."

"Exactly how old are you?" Podkin asked, forgetting it was rude to do so. He blushed as Paz glared at him.

Mo laughed. "Old enough," she said. "And there are others here much older than me."

Piles of cooked egg were scraped onto pieces of bread, and the Wardens all gathered around the fire to eat together. Pook crawled over to share his food with Pocka, and the pair of them got covered in crumbs and mess, laughing at each other in the process.

When everyone had eaten their fill, the breakfast things were cleared away and the Wardens all gathered in a loose circle around the fire pit, with their staffs, horned headdresses, and cloaks.

"We go," said Mo Grim.

"All of us?" Podkin asked.

"Yes." Mo Grim bowed her head to him. "This is a special day. We Wardens have waited many years for this."

She turned and led the others out in a procession, Podkin and Paz trotting to keep pace. Pook rode on Paz's shoulders, turning to wave and coo at his new friend, Pocka, who was himself being carried by his mother.

The strange column of rabbits headed up, out of the warren, through the mossy clearing, and into the forest.

—⁓—

The Grimwode was still thrumming with life as they marched through it. This time Podkin stared even closer at the trees, marveling at how old they must be. In the distant green shadows between the trunks, he thought he could spot shapes moving: a herd of deer, led by a stag with wide, sweeping antlers; hunched, stalking shapes that could be wolves.

He thought back to that saber-toothed beast that had almost eaten them and shuddered. At least they were safe now. No wolf would dare come near the nine giant Wardens of the forest. It made Podkin wonder if there was anything that *could* hurt them. He thought of the Gorm: their metal machines were chewing their way through the trees, even as they walked. Did the Wardens know about that? What would happen if they got as far in as the Grimwode? He felt as though they should be warned.

"Mo Grim," Podkin called, "did you know there are rabbits—evil rabbits—trying to cut down the forest? They have these horrible things made of metal with teeth and axes and grinders—"

"We know," said Mo Grim, her voice low and sad. "The forest cries out. Gormalech tries to break the Balance again."

"Is there anything you can do to stop them? Can you call on Hern for help? Can't the forest fight back with its beasts and things?"

Mo Grim stopped to lay a paw against the roots of the towering oak they were walking under. "Hern knows," she said. "He is angry. The forest *is* fighting back. It has sent you three."

The Warden chief bent down to stare at Podkin. Her eyes were deep, as brown as the soft forest earth that fed the trees all around. Podkin saw himself reflected in them.

He was a tiny, semi-earless scrap of a thing, and yet *he* was Hern's defense for the entire forest? He didn't want to criticize a god, but it didn't seem like Hern had thought things through properly.

Mo Grim bowed her head to him all the same, and the procession continued, heading north, winding in and out of the trees until they reached another clearing.

This one was filled with some kind of wooden structure. A circular fence, about twenty-five feet high. It wasn't until Podkin got closer that he realized it was made of trees. A ring of them had grown together, their branches entwining, weaving, and fusing into one solid circle of wood.

But the trees were long dead now. The leafless branches and trunks had been stripped of bark and carved all over with figures, runes, and odd picture-like glyphs. There were horned rabbits, wolves, bears, and stags, along with all the other creatures of the forest. Bees, squirrels, insects, spiders, and images of berries, pinecones, and nuts. Every inch of wood was decorated, waxed, and polished to a gleaming, honey-colored glow. It must have been the work of years; centuries, even.

"Oakhenge," said Mo Grim as they arrived. All the Wardens bowed their heads. Podkin and Paz copied.

"It's beautiful," said Paz, reaching out a paw to touch one of the carved trunks.

"It is a special place," said Mo Grim. "We go inside now."

Bending low to fit through a gap between two trunks, Mo Grim walked into the wooden circle. The other Wardens followed, as did Podkin, Paz, and Pook.

They emerged into a circular space with more carvings around the inside. In the center was another ancient tree, although this one still had one or two leaves on its branches and even the odd acorn. Its trunk was impossibly wide. *It must be a thousand years old at least*, Podkin thought.

The Wardens all gathered around it, leaving a space for Podkin and the others to approach. They looked at the small rabbits expectantly.

"Here," said Mo Grim, "is the Gift of Hern's Holt."

For a moment, Podkin thought she meant the tree itself; then he noticed — about forty feet up the trunk — something poking through the living wood. It was a small set of antlers, jutting out of the bark. They must have been placed there centuries ago, and the tree had grown around them as it slowly, ponderously aged.

"Those horns?" Podkin asked, scratching his ear stump. They didn't seem very impressive to him.

"They are part of a crown," Mo Grim explained. "Blodcrun: the horned crown of Hern's Holt."

"Why is it in a tree?"

"It was placed inside Oakhenge many, many years ago," said Mo Grim. "This tree was just a sapling then. As it grew, it swallowed the crown up. Nobody has been able to remove it, although many have tried."

"Didn't your people want to use the Gift?" Paz asked. The twelve magical items had been granted to tribes by the Goddess herself. Letting one get enveloped by a tree didn't seem like a very good way to take care of something so precious.

"We could not use it," said Mo Grim. "We could not understand what it was for."

"It doesn't have a power?" Until now, Podkin had seen four Gifts—Starclaw, Moonfyre, Ailfew, and Surestrike —and each of them had a special ability. He didn't think the Goddess would make one that didn't do *anything*.

"It does," said Mo Grim. "But we never found out what it was."

Podkin and Paz shared a look. The Gifts had been given out thousands of years ago, back when there were just twelve tribes of rabbits. If the forest Wardens hadn't figured out what the crown did in all that time, what hope did the two of them have?

There was a long period of silence as the Wardens stared at Podkin and Paz and Podkin and Paz stared at the tree with the crown's horns poking out.

"Well?" Mo Grim finally spoke. "Are you going to take the Gift? It has been foretold that you will claim it."

"Oh, right," said Podkin. He looked up the tree trunk,

then at Paz again, and swallowed. How was he supposed to even reach it? Could he ask Mo Grim for a boost? And how would he get it out of the tree when no one else had been able to? *Help me out, Goddess,* he silently prayed. *This is supposed to be part of your plan, after all.*

"I've got an idea, Pod." Paz put a hand on his shoulder and held up Ailfew. "Maybe I can use this?"

"Yes!" Podkin could have kissed her. The sickle allowed Paz to control plants and trees just by thinking about them. Maybe she could get the tree to drop the crown?

He stood back as Paz knelt at the foot of the tree. She lifted Ailfew and closed her eyes, using her mind to feel the growing, living thing before her. She frowned. It was so old, its roots so deep, and yet there was hardly a glimmer of life inside the whole thing.

"Can you do it, Paz?" Podkin whispered. The Wardens were all staring at them, expecting a miracle. This could end up being very embarrassing . . .

"I think so," said Paz, frowning. "There's not much of the tree left alive. Just a sliver. If I *push* . . ."

There was a low, creaking sound. Slowly, so slowly, the bark of the ancient oak began to twist and move. Podkin looked up to where the horns of the crown jutted out. They were beginning to tremble: a tiny bit at first, and then a definite twitch.

"It's working, Paz!"

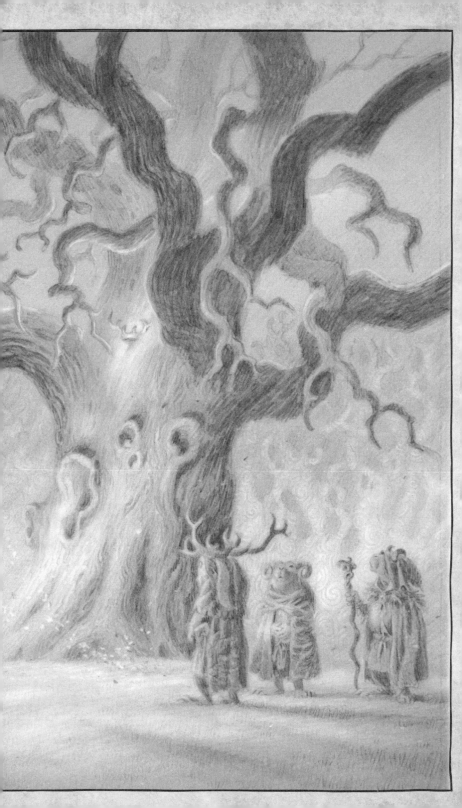

Podkin laid a hand on his sister's shoulder, hoping it would give her strength somehow. Her eyes were scrunched shut, her brow wrinkled in concentration. The crown twitched again and gradually began to emerge from the wood around it.

It was like watching some alien plant burst from the soil. The prongs of the antlers seemed to grow, getting longer and longer. Then the headpiece appeared, joining the two horns together. Finally, with a creaking pop, the tree spat the crown free, and it tumbled down for Podkin to catch.

He held it up, admiring the delicate workmanship that attached the bone antlers to a circular silver crown decorated all over with twirling vines. The Wardens all gaped, then spoke together in their language of hoots and howls. They fell to their knees, bowing their heads to the forest floor.

"Thanks," Podkin whispered to his sister. They had at least managed to get the crown free. Even though the Wardens were going to be very disappointed when they discovered he had no idea how to get the thing working.

"Well?" Paz whispered back. "What are you waiting for? Try it on!"

"Me?" Podkin said. He turned it over in his hands

again. It *did* look like it was about the right size for his head. Would the Wardens mind if he put on their Gift?

They were all staring at him again, eyes expectant. *I suppose there's nothing else to do*, he thought.

Turning so his back was to the tree, Podkin raised the crown high, then brought it down onto his head. It was a perfect fit, the circlet resting on his brow, the antlers stretching out on either side of his head, as if he were a miniature version of the Wardens themselves.

"I don't think it does any—" he started to say.

Then it happened.

From nowhere, into his head, his mind, came a flood of *everything*.

Emotions, images, sensations, sounds, scents—incredible, overpowering scents—it all rushed into his brain, too fast for him to handle.

<**Curious**, *head tingling* [rich, coppery blood], (rabbit smell), SOMETHING WRONG.>

Podkin reached his paws up to try to pull the crown from his head, try to stop all this *noise* that was flooding in. But the thing wouldn't budge, and it all continued. Something else, something *other* was inside his brain, as puzzled as he was by what was going on.

<**Irritated**, *flea bites inside head* [blood taste still], (rabbit smell close by).>

He could hear himself screaming, feel Paz's hands trying to get the crown off as well. The thing in his brain was searching, trying to find him. Podkin had the sensation of four paws, claws sinking into soft forest dirt. His mouth was bigger, longer: wide and hungry and . . . fanged.

<**Understand**, *flea in head familiar* [little rabbit blood], (there, inside the tree thing).>

"Stop!" Podkin managed to shout. He fell to the ground, trying to scrape the crown off against the tree roots. There was hooting and barking all around him as the Wardens began to panic, but all he could think of was the thing in his head. It was so close to discovering him now, he could feel it narrowing its attention until all its senses were focused on Podkin in a sudden moment of understanding.

<(YOU).>

Looking through the gaps in Oakhenge, Podkin saw the saber-toothed wolf from the forest. It stood by a tree trunk, staring at him with those knowing, amber eyes. And yet — with a sensation that made his little head spin — Podkin felt he was looking at *himself* at the same time.

Frightened rabbit/wolf/frightened rabbit/wolf. It was too much for him to cope with. With a final squeak, he passed out, into Paz's arms.

Pack

When Podkin woke up again, he was lying on the floor of Oakhenge, his head in Paz's lap. The Wardens were clustered around, bending over to peer at him and make concerned noises. He could also hear Pook shouting "Doggy! Doggy!" He sounded very excited.

"Podkin, you're awake!" Paz pulled him upright and gave him a squeeze. "What happened?"

"My head..." Podkin managed to say. "Something in it..."

He turned to see where the wolf had gone, and he almost fainted again when he saw it only a few yards away, sitting on its haunches—actually inside Oakhenge—staring at him.

119

"Doggy! Doggy!" Pook shouted again, tottering over to grab at the wolf's furry paw and cuddle it.

"Pook, no!" Podkin shouted. "It's a *wolf*, not a doggy!" But the wolf just lowered its nose to sniff the baby rabbit, then looked up to stare at Podkin again.

"It's all right, Pod," said Paz. "Rake knows the wolf. I think he's friends with it."

"*Du spakk mit der wulf?*" Rake was standing nearby, staring at Podkin with great interest. He repeated his question, pointing at the wolf, then Podkin.

"Rake speaks only a few words of Gott," explained Mo Grim. "He is asking if you spoke to the wolf."

"Spoke to it?" Podkin said. "In a way. I think it was in my head."

The noises and sensations had gone, but that was because the crown of Blodcrun was now in his lap. It must have fallen off while he was unconscious.

Mo Grim said something to Rake in their forest language. There was an excited exchange of grunts, clicks, and yowls.

"Rake can tell the wolf knows you," said Mo Grim. "He can't speak with it directly, but he senses you can. You two have a connection."

"What . . . what kind of wolf is it?" Podkin asked. Never mind connections—the very thought that something wild and dangerous was staring at him so intensely made him feel like running for the nearest burrow.

"Rake calls the beast Truefang," Mo Grim said. "He says it is the alpha male of a pack that lives in the Grimwode. The wolves here are different. Much bigger and more fierce. An ancient breed."

Truefang's eyes didn't leave Podkin for an instant. When Mo Grim had finished speaking, the wolf bent his head to the fallen crown and nudged it with his nose.

"I think it wants you to put the crown on again," said Paz. Even she was trembling slightly. Podkin could feel her shaking against his back.

"I don't think I want to," Podkin said, remembering that awful flood of sensations. He was quite sure wolf thoughts and rabbit thoughts weren't meant to mix. As if sensing his reluctance, Truefang nudged the crown again.

"I think you'd better," said Paz. "You don't want to make a two-ton, saber-toothed wolf angry, do you?"

Podkin gulped and reached for Blodcrun. Wincing against the overpowering rush of feelings, he put it back on his head.

—*You. Small rabbit.*

It didn't seem too bad this time. Perhaps because he was prepared for the unsettling feeling of seeing himself through the wolf's mind. There was still the massive rush of thoughts and sensations, but if he didn't think about it too much, it all swam together into something like language.

Wolves didn't speak in words, of course, but Podkin found his mind could take all the images and scents Truefang was transmitting and change them into something he could understand. He was thinking in wolf.

— *Greetings*, Podkin sent to Truefang

— *Greetings*, the wolf sent back. He gave Podkin's foot a lick.

Podkin wondered how they could be talking to each other in this way.

Something to do with the crown, of course, but how was it working? He could feel the question being sent to Truefang. The wolf answered with a picture: a scene of itself licking Podkin's blood, back when Podkin, Paz, and Pook were fleeing Vetch.

"My blood," Podkin said aloud.

"What?" said Paz. "Your blood?"

"Yes," said Podkin. "That's how the crown works! It lets you speak to animals, but they have to taste your blood first. Truefang licked mine when we met him the other night!"

Mo Grim gave a cry of wonder and started telling the

other Wardens. They all cheered as well — the mystery of their Gift had finally been solved.

"Ask him what happened to Vetch," said Paz. "Did he eat him?"

Podkin made a mental picture of the ginger-furred Vetch and sent it to Truefang. The wolf gave a rumbling growl and sent back a picture of the rabbit fleeing down the cart track to Silverock, his exotic cloak flapping behind him.

"No," translated Podkin. "He escaped. Looks like he headed south."

"What about Crom and the others?"

Truefang listened to Podkin's thoughts, then sent back an image of an empty camp. The faint scent of Crom's leather armor, mixed with wood smoke, lingered over everything.

"They've gone," Podkin said. "The camp is empty."

"Did they go back to Dark Hollow, do you think?" Paz asked. Podkin had no idea how to ask that question; he just felt a sudden rush of loneliness and longing for his friends. But that was enough for Truefang to understand. He sent Podkin a picture of the cart track again, this time shimmering with smears of different colors. It took Podkin a few moments to realize what they were.

Trails? Scents? he asked Truefang, and the wolf gave a

small huff of agreement. This was how the forest must look to a creature with such an amazing sense of smell. Anything that lived left trails of its passing behind on everything it touched. Trails that a wolf could read like a book. It was as if Podkin's eyes had been opened to a whole new, invisible world.

That track there was Crom's. There were thick, heavy marks of scent where his feet had walked, and smaller ones on leaves and branches higher up where he had been brushing his fingers to guide himself.

The shimmering silver markings were Yarrow's. Podkin could smell the mix of patchouli and lavender he liked to dab behind his ears. The other scents must be Dodge, Rill, and Tansy. They were less familiar to Podkin, but he could pick up a trace of the nettle tea Rill liked to drink and Tansy's burnt fur, singed from working alongside Sorrel at the hot forge.

"They headed south as well." Podkin translated the image to Paz. "They must have followed Vetch's trail."

"Maybe they thought he had us?" said Paz. She sounded worried—upset at the thought her friends might have carried on without them.

"They would not have been able to find your tracks," said Mo Grim. "Rake hid every mark you made. The trail of this Vetch would have been the only one left for them to see."

"I hope they caught him," said Podkin. The sudden rush of anger he felt made Starclaw buzz at his side and Truefang curl his lip and growl.

"Can we follow them?" Paz asked. "I mean — now that we've rescued the crown for you, and discovered what it does . . . are we free to go? Or do we have to stay here . . . ?"

She didn't want to say "as prisoners," but the thought was in her head. Mo Grim had said something about a war, but not when and where it was going to be fought. What if it was years from now? What if they had to wait for the Gorm to plow through all the forest until they reached the Grimwode?

"You must do as you wish," said Mo Grim. "Hern and the Goddess are leading you. If it is your will to follow your friends, then we will come with you."

"What about the Gorm?" Podkin asked. "Don't you want us to fight them?"

At the mention of their enemy, Truefang snarled again. Podkin's head was filled with a sudden rush of fury. It made his fur prickle, his teeth gnash. He could smell the stink of hot iron and the smoke of burning trees. The screeching and grating of metal filled his ears. The wolf knew the Gorm and could feel their wrongness much more keenly than Podkin ever had. In turn, Podkin found himself showing the wolf everything he knew about the twisted, poisoned rabbits. All the fear he had felt in running from them. The terror and the danger of battling Scramashank in the snow and on Ancients' Island. It made Truefang want to fight and tear: a great, primal rage that was completely overpowering.

Before he knew what he was doing, Podkin found himself on all fours, snarling and snapping. Truefang was doing the same. Even though the pair of them made a very comical couple, Paz found herself stepping back, pulling Pook with her. She could feel the anger washing off them in waves.

Finally, Truefang and Podkin both raised their heads and howled at the sky. It was a piercing, haunting sound that echoed between the trees of the ancient forest around them.

Almost instantly there came an answering howl, then another, and another. Moments later, a second saber-toothed wolf came trotting through a gap in the woven trees, sniffing the air and staring at them all with its hungry amber eyes. It was followed by a third, and a fourth. Soon the inside of the henge was full of shaggy, furry bodies, jostling and snuffling. At least twenty wolves with every shade of dapple-gray fur. Young, old, male, female. Truefang had called the pack, and now they were there, ready for their alpha's command.

Podkin, having finished howling, felt the animal rage

ebb away. He was still on all fours and had a dim memory of snapping his teeth and growling. It was a little embarrassing, at least until he noticed all the wolves that were suddenly surrounding him.

— *Pack. Fight.* Truefang sent him something that was more a feeling than an image. It was the sense of family and unity that his pack gave him. That and a hint of the wish he had to rip and tear the Gorm from his beloved forest.

"What's happening, Pod?" Paz asked. She was clutching Pook to her chest and trying to ignore him as he made his own little growling and howling noises.

"This is Truefang's pack," Podkin said. "I think they want to help us fight the Gorm."

As if in answer, all twenty wolves raised their noses and howled at the sky together. The Wardens joined in — so did Pook — and the forest was filled with the sound for miles around.

Interlude

Sythica raises a hand, and the bard stops midtale, his head tilted up as if he is about to howl like a wolf himself. The bonedancers all turn their eyes to their Mother Superior, leaving Rue as the only one still lost in the story, still hearing the cries of the wolf pack as they fade into the quiet stillness of the forest.

"Is there a problem?" the bard asks. He is hoping this isn't the part where he gets pushed backwards into the weasel pit.

"No," replies Sythica. "Your tale is adequate. It is simply time for our ritual."

"Adequate," mutters the bard. "Thank you so much."

He watches warily as his audience of bonedancers all reach into the leather pouches at their belts and draw out a termite or beetle. They hold them up as an offering and, as one, reach across with their other hands to twist off the insects' heads. The dead creatures are then thrown to the floor in a patter of shells and twitching thoraxes.

"Well," says the bard, once the bonedancers have finished, "I must say that's a relief. If you've all killed something today, then you probably won't be killing me."

"I haven't killed anything yet," says Sythica, making the bard freeze in midchuckle. She watches with a twinkle in her eyes as the bard gulps and blinks for a moment, then makes a gesture to her sisters. The bonedancers all stand and begin to leave the chamber in rows.

"Is it over?" Rue calls out, jumping from his seat and wringing his paws. "Don't say it's over! The story isn't finished yet!"

Sythica turns her masked face to the little rabbit. When she speaks, her voice is almost kindly. Or at least slightly less threatening than usual. "It is not over, little bard. We are just stopping for lunch. You will be led back to your chamber to eat."

With that, their bonedancer escorts reappear and shepherd Rue and the bard back to their cell. Someone has already put out a simple meal of dandelion leaves and diced radish for them, and once they are inside, the bonedancers shut and lock the door, leaving them alone.

Without saying a word, the pair of them sit down on one of the beds and begin sharing the food.

They eat in silence for a while, crunching leaves the only sound. The bard is just beginning to wonder why Rue is being so quiet when the little rabbit suddenly bursts into tears.

"Rue!" says the bard. "What's wrong?"

"They're going to kill you!" Rue wails. "They hate your story and they're going to throw you in the weasel pit!"

"Now, now," says the bard. "Don't . . . um . . . cry." He hasn't had much experience with emotional children. Thinking he should do something, he pats his apprentice's shoulder. Rue instantly throws himself into the bard's arms and begins to dribble tears and snot on his tunic.

"You're going to be torn to pieces! The weasel will chew off your ears and suck out your eyeballs!"

"All right, all right!" says the bard. "Less of the blood and gore . . . You're starting to make me nervous! Look. Nothing's going to happen to me — I think. They seem to be liking the story fine."

Rue pauses in his sobbing to look up at the bard with red-rimmed, weepy eyes. "No, they don't. They think it's rotten. All they do is sit and stare. I haven't heard one laugh or cry or anything."

"That's true," says the bard. "But they're different from

any rabbits you've met before. I'm pretty sure they like my tale. They haven't walked out on me, at least. I've had much worse audiences than this, you know."

"Really?" Rue says. It's quite clear he doesn't believe a word of it.

"Oh, yes," says the bard. "It's when they start throwing things that you have to worry." He gives Rue another shoulder pat for good measure. "It'll be fine; you'll see."

"But aren't you worried? Aren't you nervous?"

"Well," says the bard, "I have to admit I am a little nervous *now*, after you brought up the eyeball-sucking thing."

"I'm sorry." Rue looks as though he is about to start crying again.

"I was joking!" the bard says. "Although it's true — I am a bit nervous. I always am when I have to perform. Every bard is. You wouldn't be any good if you weren't. Admittedly, your life isn't always at stake, but even so, it's hard to speak in front of a group of rabbits you don't know. What if they laugh at you? What if you forget your words or stutter? What if you trip over your feet and land on your face?"

"All bards get nervous?" Rue asks.

"Of course. But then you start the song or the story, and soon you're lost in the performance. You can see the audience looking up at you. You can see them captured by the spell you're weaving. And then it's over, and you get the applause. Maybe even a mug of ale. That makes it all worth it."

"Except the bonedancers haven't applauded you."

"No."

"And all they gave you was some water and some vegetables."

"Yes."

"And they're thinking about feeding you to their weasel."

"That too." The bard sighs. "Thanks, Rue. You really know how to build a rabbit up. Trust me, though. It's going to be all right. I promise. Now, finish your lunch before we have to go back."

With a few more sniffs and snuffles, Rue climbs off the bard's lap and starts eating again. The bard watches him, hoping that it *is* going to be all right. The Goddess would be looking out for him, after all, wouldn't she? He offers a silent prayer, just in case.

A few minutes later, their door is unlocked and the bonedancers lead them back to the hall.

———

Sythica and the ranks of bonedancers are already there, sitting motionless in their semicircle around the hall's edge.

The bard takes his place center stage, trying to ignore the skittering sound of claws on the stone floor of the pit behind him. Rue has hopped into his place on the end of the front bench and is looking at him with those big, worried eyes. The bard feels the urge to run screaming back to his cell, but he manages to swallow it and instead gives his apprentice a wink. This is what he does best. He's done it a thousand, thousand times before. He's going to be fine.

"Are you ready to continue?" Sythica asks him, her voice echoing around the chamber.

"I am," says the bard. His voice wobbles only slightly.

"Before you do," Sythica interrupts, "I have a question. Something we were discussing over lunch."

"Yes?"

"You said in your story that Paz discovered tribes had female chiefs long before the tradition of first sons became the norm."

"She did."

"Naturally, as a female order, we find this very interesting. But we thought Chief Thorn-Singer was the first rabbit to break the old custom."

"She was," says the bard. "Paz is — I mean she became — Chief Thorn-Singer. Much later on than this tale, of course."

Sythica nods, taking this in. "Impressive," she says. "She would have made a good bonedancer."

133

"Many people thought so," says the bard.

"Did they, now?" Sythica's eyes twinkle as she snaps up his comment. "You seem to know an awful lot about all this. Are you sure it is just one of your stories?"

The bard blinks for a moment, wondering whether to tell them that he is, or was, Pook Lopkinson, brother of Paz and Podkin. He decides not to: *Always best to save your plot twists for the end,* he reminds himself. Besides, that could be a useful piece of information should they decide to turn him into weasel food.

"A story, yes," he says. "Some might say a legend. But every legend has a fragment of truth in it. This one more so, as I have researched it very carefully and kept it as close to the real events as I can."

"Very well," says Sythica. It sounds as though she is smiling behind her mask. "Please continue. Truefang's pack had just agreed to help Podkin, had they not?"

"They had," says the bard. "And they were not the only ones."

Scramashank Rides Out

Once Truefang and his wolves had accompanied the rabbits back to Hern's Holt, Rake told them of two other packs that lived in the Grimwode. He was sure they also would want to join the growing forest army.

Over the next two days, Podkin traveled to meet them, each time using Starclaw to nick one of his fingers and offer blood to the packs' alpha wolves, Deadeye and Nightclaw. One lick, and they shared his mind, just as Truefang had done. Both packs knew of the Gorm and were filled with a deep, snarling hatred for them that went back to the days when Gormalech surrounded the Grimwode with his seething metal body.

With Truefang's grays, Deadeye's black wolves, and

Nightclaw's brown furs fully assembled, Podkin and Paz decided it was best to head for Sparrowfast. Crom would be there, maybe also their mother, by now. Their Uncle Hennic was bound to be impressed with their new troops and would *definitely* let them have the bow. With that, and all the soldier rabbits they could muster, surely they stood a good chance against the Gorm.

Podkin prayed that they did.

With a final, howling farewell to the Grimwode, the children, the Wardens, and more than sixty hulking, saber-toothed wolves headed out.

They filled the gaps between the trees as they marched: a weaving sea of fur and glowing eyes. In Podkin's head, three voices babbled, showing him gleaming twines of scent and relaying every tiny noise from miles around. It was too much information at first, until he learned to channel the flow. He pictured doors closing in his head, allowing him to control which wolf he shared minds with. Even so, it was a sensation he could not get used to. Most of the time, he kept the Blodcrun horns stored safely in his pack and his thoughts nice and secret, just the way he liked them.

The Wardens marched in the middle of their wolfish escort, Podkin and Paz among them. Pook had taken a shine to Truefang, and to Podkin's surprise, the alpha wolf let Pook ride on his back. The little rabbit sat on the wolf's shoulders, clutching handfuls of gray hair and raising his tiny nose to the sky to howl every now and then.

"I a wolf! I a wolf!" he kept shouting.

The whole throng headed down through the forest, using tracks that the Wardens seemed to know well. As they moved farther from the Grimwode, the trees became smaller and smaller, until they looked almost spindly. *How strange*, Podkin thought. *When we first came into the forest, every tree seemed massive to me. Now these ordinary ones look like tiny copies of what they should be.*

The journey took them three days and two nights, which they spent camping in clearings with springs of fresh water running nearby. The Wardens slept on the forest floor under their cloaks, but they brought a small tent for Podkin, Paz, and Pook to sleep in. Podkin wasn't surprised to wake each morning and find that Pook had crawled out to lie next to Truefang, curled up under the big wolf's paw, among the litter of chewed bones from deer that the wolves had hunted in the night.

"You really shouldn't do that, Pook," he told his brother. "That wolf might wake up in the night, fancying a snack, and forget that you're supposed to be his friend."

"I a wolf!" Pook replied, pretending to chew on a bone.

By dawn on the third day, they were creeping past the tiny warren of Stumphaven, the wolves flowing over its mound and past its entrance doors on silent, padded paws.

Luckily, the rabbits were all fast asleep inside and had no idea a sea of predators was washing over their heads as they dreamed.

From there it was only a few hours' march along the forest edge to Silverock. And beyond that, a clear run to Sparrowfast, if Podkin remembered the maps they had studied in Dark Hollow correctly.

As they neared the mound of Silverock, Podkin started to grow more and more excited at the thought of seeing his friends again. Would they be at Sparrowfast, expecting them? Or would they think them dead? Would Mother be there yet? What would she do when she found out they had let Pook make best friends with something that could eat him in one bite?

———

The story of the day that Grimheart Forest woke and sent its army out to war is one that will be passed down from rabbit to rabbit through generations.

By the seventh day that Podkin, Paz, and Pook had been missing, Crom and the others had spent two days following Vetch's trail, only to lose it at the very edge of the forest.

Not knowing what to do, they had headed for the nearest warren, Silverock, and asked the chieftain for help.

Chief Agbert had been very understanding. He let them stay and even helped them to run daily search parties into the forest. The children's mother and the main party of Dark Hollow rabbits had also arrived and learned the terrible news. Everyone, except for Brigid, was in a state of shock, thinking they would never see the little ones again. The mission to Sparrowfast was completely forgotten, and then word came that Chief Hennic's rabbits were coming to *them*. The entire warren.

The little messenger bird that had brought the news had only a tiny piece of parchment. Help us. We are fleeing, it had said. The Gorm are here.

Wondering what it meant, Chief Agbert had summoned the whole warren, along with the recent arrivals from Dark Hollow. The entire group of rabbits were gathered outside the entrance gates, ready to welcome Sparrowfast, when a shout went up.

"The north! Look to the north!"

The rabbits all turned their heads to where the deep, green cloud of Grimheart Forest stretched into the horizon. There, pouring from the forest's edge, was a sight fit for the most bizarre of legends. Wolves — huge ones, fanged ones: sixty or more in every shade of gray, brown, and black.

At first, the rabbits rubbed their eyes and shook their heads. Then they started to scream and wail. Then they noticed something else among the tide of fur and teeth: giant, horned figures striding toward them with sweeping cloaks made of leaves, webs, and brambles.

"It's the Beast of Grimheart!" a shout went up. Then another voice cried, "The Beast *and* all his family *and* a pack of giant wolves!" The rabbit warriors of Silverock and Dark Hollow drew their weapons and tried to form a shield wall. It was tricky, as most of them were still staring, mouths gaping open.

Among the army of wolves and beasts, Pook was riding on Truefang's back. Podkin and Paz were running alongside to keep up.

"Podkin, look!" Paz shouted over the panting, growling din of the superpack. "There's a whole bunch of rabbits outside Silverock!"

"What are they doing?" Podkin called back. He could see the warren mound of Silverock, the rows and rows of wooden beehives in their neat little fenced enclosures, and, by the entrance doors, a crowd of rabbits who looked as if they were all about to have heart attacks at the same time.

"I don't know," Paz replied. "Some kind of ceremony, looks like. Put your crown on!"

"Why?" Podkin said.

"It'll look amazing!" Paz grinned at him, and he found himself grinning back.

They'll think we're some kind of wild hunt from the forest, he thought, pulling the crown onto his head. *I'm going to be part of a real-life fairy tale!* His excitement instantly transmitted to the three alphas, who howled, setting off all sixty wolves.

"Awwooo!" Pook shouted beside them, making Podkin and Paz laugh. The next thing Podkin knew, Deadeye, the black-furred pack leader, was behind him, scooping him up with his nose and flipping him up to ride on his shoulders like Pook. Nightclaw, the other alpha, did the same to Paz. The three of them pulled ahead of the pack, leading the throng, all of them cheering and waving at the startled rabbits before them.

It was Yarrow who spotted the little rabbits first, just as the Silverock warriors were getting ready with their spears. "It's Podkin!" he yelled. "And Paz and Pook! Look, there! Riding on the wolves!"

Podkin's mother, standing with Chief Agbert, let out a shriek. The other Dark Hollow rabbits peered closer, then began to cheer. Instead of running in terror from the approaching wolves, they started dancing and shouting. The Silverock rabbits didn't know what to do. Swords and spears were lowered, but not too much, and they stood back as all the rabbits of Dark Hollow rushed to meet the new arrivals: Podkin, Paz, and Pook; wolf riders; lords of the forest.

And all the time, Brigid stood quietly watching, a smile on her face, alongside Yarrow the bard, who had both paws clutched to his head, frantically trying to remember every single tiny detail of the best homecoming scene a bard could ever hope for.

―⁓―

After the three little rabbits had been thoroughly hugged, kissed, and cried over by everyone, the Wardens were introduced, as were the wolves. Lady Enna, usually so strong and commanding, kept hugging Podkin, Paz, and Pook and sobbing into their fur. She had been certain she would never see her children again, despite Brigid's many reassurances.

Tansy quietly took Lady Enna away for a drink of chamomile tea and a cuddle with Pook. The others gathered around Podkin and Paz, who told their tale of the last few days, with help from Mo Grim. Once they had finished, and after a long round of applause, Crom revealed what had happened to the rest of the party.

"We woke late afternoon, with our heads all groggy and spinning," he said. "As soon as we realized you were gone, we started to search the forest. We found your tracks right away, then the blood. We trailed it into the forest, but it suddenly disappeared. All we could find were Vetch's paw marks, heading south. We thought he might be carrying you somehow—nothing else made sense—so we followed them. We lost his trail in the forest around Stumphaven, damn his treacherous ginger hide. And we've been searching the forest for you ever since. We never even made it to Sparrowfast."

There was much cursing and growling about Vetch and what everyone wanted to do to him. Most of it wasn't suitable for young ears, so Brigid drew Podkin and Paz aside. She hugged them both, tears in her eyes.

"I am so sorry," she said. "I knew you would get lost along the way. I knew it would lead you to another Gift. But I had no idea Vetch would try to harm you. If I had, I would never have let you go."

"Don't worry," said Paz, hugging her back. "If it hadn't happened, we would never have met Mo Grim, and we wouldn't have the wolves on our side."

"Yes," said Podkin. "It was worth it in the end. Although it was a bit scary at the time."

"Nothing that brings harm to you is worth it," said Brigid, crying again. "It's not fair for you to face these things so young. Sometimes I wonder—"

But what she wondered was never said, as another shout went up. A second crowd of rabbits had appeared, marching in lines toward them from the west.

"What now?" Yarrow muttered to himself. "I've only

just memorized the thirty-five different shades of wolf fur. I can't be expected to deal with anything else. It's giving me a migraine."

Ignoring the moaning bard, Podkin shadowed his eyes with a paw and squinted to see what was approaching. His first horrible thought was that it might be the Gorm — he had no idea that the Silverock rabbits were expecting anybody — but Crom soon put his mind at rest.

"It's your uncle, Podkin. The rabbits from Sparrowfast are coming. Fleeing the Gorm, we think. We were here to welcome them."

It all made sense to Podkin now. He had thought it a little unusual that everyone was there as they poured out of the forest, but then, with Brigid around, you never knew . . .

He watched as the Sparrowfast rabbits drew nearer. They marched in orderly columns of warriors with ash spears and long shields painted sky blue with flocks of black sparrows silhouetted across them. The soldiers were followed by three large wagons stacked with barrels, crates, and sacks, and another covered in wooden birdcages. The fluttering shapes of hundreds of tiny sparrows could be seen inside: the messenger birds that their warren was famous for.

The wagons were followed by the rest of the Sparrow-fast rabbits, marching with their life's belongings carried in sacks on their backs and heads. The whole procession was led by a very important-looking rabbit mounted on a giant rat. Both were clad in panels of sky-blue leather armor and strutted with great authority.

As they got closer, Podkin could see that the rider had the same sandy-brown fur as his mother, and the same piercing green eyes. Those eyes that could pin you with a glare that made you want to cry and apologize, even if you hadn't done anything wrong.

Across his lap, the rider carried an enormous wooden bow carved all over with whorls and spirals. *Soulshot*, Podkin realized. *The sacred Gift of Sparrowfast Warren.*

Podkin watched as his Uncle Hennic rode up and surveyed his welcome party.

There were wolves everywhere: lounging on the warren mound, chasing one another through the meadows, and cocking their legs up against the beehives. Some curled together for a welcome nap; some stared at the newcomers with undisguised hunger in their wild eyes.

The rabbits of Silverock and Dark Hollow were clustered in groups around each of the Wardens, trying to communicate with gestures and shouts. Lady Enna was in a heap of skirts by the warren entrance, being given tea and trying to stop Pook from marking his territory up against the doorway. The only rabbits who had even noticed Hennic arrive were Podkin, Paz, Crom, and Yarrow, who was trying to count just how many spearmen there were while memorizing the exact shade of blue they had on their shields.

The chaos of the whole scene did not seem to impress Uncle Hennic. He took a good look around, his eyes seeming to glow greener with every heartbeat. He scowled so hard that Podkin could almost hear the blood throbbing in his head. Finally, he reached up to remove his helmet and then bellowed in a voice that made every set of ears —both wolf and rabbit—twitch to attention.

"What, in the name of the Goddess herself, is this sorry shambles?" He raised the magic bow and gestured at the mass of bodies before him. "Did you fools not get my message? Do you not know what it means? The Gorm are upon us, you idiots! Scramashank himself has ridden out! Did you hear me?"

He took a deep breath, stood up in his stirrups, and bellowed again in a voice that echoed to the forest trees and back.

"Call the warrens! Summon a council! Scramashank rides out!"

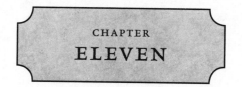

Quarrel

S ummon a council!" Chief Agbert echoed, and there
was an instant rush of rabbits trying to do several
things at once.

It took until early evening for everyone to get organized enough to call a proper "council of the tribes."
Podkin, with Rake's help, had to try to tell the wolves that
there would be no fighting yet and that the two-legged,
long-eared creatures needed to talk first. For beasts that
had no idea of talking or of waiting anything more than a
few minutes to do something, this was harder than anyone
could have imagined. Finally, the alpha wolves led their
packs off into the forest to hunt. Podkin hoped they would
remember to return.

The Sparrowfast rabbits scrabbled to put up marquees and tents outside the warren entrance. They all seemed to be very worried about their cargo of sparrows, which were upset by the upheaval. Special bird handlers fed them worms and plump grubs, while a bard with a harp played soothing music to calm them down.

The rest of the rabbits all squeezed themselves into the Silverock longburrow.

It was a large chamber, in the center of which was a gigantic granite boulder laced throughout with seams of pure silver: the rock that was uncovered by the first rabbits to dig here and from which they had taken the name of their warren.

Lucky for them it was silver they found and not a piece of Gormalech-possessed iron, Podkin thought, remembering the tale of Sandywell, the warren that had become the Gorm's home.

Curved tables surrounded the rock, with the chief's throne at the far end, next to a great stone fireplace. The walls were hung with tapestries, all seeming to be of bees and beehives, celebrating the honey mead that the warren was famous for.

Chief Agbert took his place on his throne, flanked by Chief Hennic and Lady Enna (with Pook cradled on her lap). Other rabbits pushed and shoved, trying to sit as close to the leaders as possible. Podkin found himself herded around the circle until he was next to Paz and Crom, about twenty seats from his mother.

There was a tense atmosphere, with each tribe giving the others stares and wary glances. A crackling, brooding energy, just like the air before a thunderstorm. *Maybe this is why the tribes don't come together very often*, Podkin thought.

He looked at the smartly dressed Sparrowfast rabbits in their blue-and-black armor; the rich, proud Silverocks; and the ragtag, half-starved mismatches of Dark Hollow. Where would the first quarrel come from? His mother and her brother, Hennic, were both staring straight ahead, brows furrowed, mouths set. Podkin thought he might have a good idea about the answer to that question.

"Everyone keeps looking at us funny," Paz whispered to him. "They don't think we should be this close to the chieftains."

Podkin looked to the far end of the hall where some little tables had been set out for the children. Most of them looked about the same age as him; some were even older. The other rabbits probably thought they were naughty kittens who had wandered away from their given places.

"You stay where you are," said Crom, guessing Podkin's thoughts. "You have as much right to be here as any other rabbit." He stretched his arm around Podkin and

Paz, putting on his fiercest warrior stare. All the rabbits who had been glaring at them seemed to suddenly look away.

"Thanks, Crom," Podkin whispered.

Chief Agbert stood up and cleared his throat.

"Welcome, all, to Silverock. Our home is your home, and please forgive the crush. We are not used to hosting so many visitors at once. This whole gathering has been very . . . unexpected." His eyes lingered on the forest Wardens, who were taking up a whole table to themselves, squatting on chairs that looked as though they were about to snap into splinters under their weight.

There was a polite ripple of applause from everyone gathered, and then he continued.

"This, however, is not a social event. The threat of the Gorm has reached our side of the forest, and we are all in danger. Our neighbors at Sparrowfast Warren have been attacked—as have many others here, I know—but seeing as the Gorm are currently in his warren, perhaps Chief Hennic would like to speak to us all first?"

Hennic had clearly been expecting this and stood instantly, clearing his throat. Podkin couldn't help noticing his mother roll her eyes.

"Thank you, Chief Agbert, for your hospitality and aid. Sparrowfast will not forget your kindness.

"It is true, as you say. We have been attacked. Two days

ago we received a sparrow from Oakbud Hollow, a small warren to the west of us. They said a Gorm force had been spotted marching at full speed around the forest edge. We sent out a scouting party immediately. Only one of them returned."

Hennic pointed a finger to the edge of the longburrow where a wounded rabbit sat hunched in a chair, his head and left arm covered in bandages.

"He told of a large force: two hundred Gorm warriors and riders. Among them was a tall rabbit with a helmet of crooked horns — Scramashank himself — and another upon a black rat: a witch-rabbit who wielded a magic staff that could call down lightning from the sky. She blew our scouting party to bits in seconds."

At the mention of Scramashank, the whole long-burrow shuddered, but when Hennic described the witch, Podkin felt Crom clutch his hand tightly. The blind warrior even began to tremble — just a tiny jitter — but Podkin could feel it through his paw, and it was growing.

Podkin looked up at Crom's face, wondering what Hennic had said that could have affected him so. Then he remembered Crom's tale about how he had lost his sight. Hadn't that been at the hands of a witch-rabbit? Hadn't she used some kind of lightning magic as well?

"We knew they were heading for us," Hennic contin-ued. "We knew that we couldn't fight them on our own.

We made the impossible decision to leave our warren and run. Our beautiful home . . ."

The Sparrowfast rabbits all hung their heads. Some of them began to sob; others wiped tears from their eyes.

"But with your help, we might stand a chance. With Silverock beside us, we can fight back. Destroy the Gorm once and for all . . ."

There was a murmur around the longburrow, along with quite a few shaking heads. The rabbits of Silverock didn't sound too keen on that plan, and Podkin couldn't help noticing Hennic hadn't even *mentioned* Dark Hollow.

"Chief Hennic, thank you." Agbert stood and nodded at the other chieftain, waiting for him to sit down. Hennic glared, and for a moment Podkin thought he was going to ignore his host, but finally he took his seat again, growling as he did so.

"We have heard the tragic tale of Sparrowfast," said Agbert, "and you have our sympathy. But we also have another warren here, along with their . . . um . . . allies. Lady Enna, would you care to speak before the council?"

Podkin bit his lip as his mother got up. She was still weak and scarred by her ordeal at the hands of the Gorm, but she stood as proud as ever—a gleam in her eye that easily matched Hennic's.

She handed Pook to Auntie Olwyn, who was sitting behind her, and turned back to the longburrow.

"I am Lady Enna, once of Munbury Warren," she said. Her voice rang out clearly, making even the children at the back of the hall look up. "Our home there was taken, my husband . . . killed. Since then we have been living in the forest, in Dark Hollow Warren. We have no chief at the moment but have chosen a council of war." She waved a paw to indicate the seats where Podkin, Paz, Crom, Rill, and Dodge were sitting. "And they have asked me to speak for them.

"Like Sparrowfast . . . my brother's . . . warren, we have come asking for help. We are also fighting the Gorm, but through a different means.

"As you might have seen earlier, my son and daughter have brought with them the forces of the forest. They did this because they have been chosen by the Goddess herself —and Hern, too, it would seem—to defeat their ancient enemy."

A murmur of wonder rippled through the hall at this. Ears and eyes twitched in Podkin's direction, and he blushed under his fur. He felt rather than saw Paz straighten her shoulders beside him. His mother waited a few moments for quiet before continuing.

"All know the story of the Balance. Of how the Goddess and her sister tricked Gormalech under the ground, and how he is now trying to return by using enslaved rabbits as his weapon.

"All know as well the story of the twelve tribes and the Gifts they were given. My children have been collecting these, with the Goddess's blessing, and plan to use them to strike back, to return the Balance to the way it should be.

"They already had four of the Twelve Gifts, and they have now found a horned crown named Blodcrun: a Gift that has been hidden away in the depths of Grimheart Forest.

"We have used the sacred hammer of Applecross to forge arrows that can pierce Gorm armor—" At this, her audience whooped and cheered. "But we have come to ask my brother for his aid. Not for his army, but for his bow.

"For our plan—and our arrows—to work, we need to use Soulshot, the Gift of Sparrowfast, to fire them. We need to engage the Gorm in battle, and then Podkin and Paz, my children, will be able to strike at Scramashank himself. This is the only chance we have to beat the Gorm. This is our only chance to save ourselves."

There were murmurs from all around the longburrow. Podkin saw rabbits staring at him, open-mouthed, trying to get a glimpse of the Gifts he bore. He no longer felt quite so small and unimportant. He heard snatches of whispered questions, the names "Blodcrun" and "Grimheart" repeated. Many seemed excited that such a thing had happened, that there might be a chance of striking back against the Gorm.

But raised voices came from the direction of the Sparrowfast rabbits. His mother's words had angered and outraged them. Take their warren's Gift? Give it to some children? Ridiculous!

Eyes began to turn to Chief Hennic. Everyone could see the rage slowly building up in him. His ears trembled with it. His clenched fists shook. Finally it exploded.

"I might have known!" he shouted. "You and your tatty bunch of criminals have come to steal my Gift! I knew the minute I saw you! You've always been jealous that I became chief! You've always wanted this bow. Give it to your scrawny one-eared brat of a child? You must be joking! He'd probably feed it to one of his pet wolves!"

"This has got nothing to do with jealousy, Hennic!" Podkin's mother turned to face her brother, paws clenched. "I couldn't care less that you became chief. This is about our survival! Do you think it makes me happy that my own beloved children are involved in this war? Podkin and Paz are the *only* ones who have ever even scratched the Gorm. They've met Scramashank and beaten him twice! They *are* our only hope. If you don't believe me, listen to our bard: he can tell you the story . . ."

"With pleasure!" Yarrow leaped up from his seat and bowed elaborately. "It's a work in progress, of course — you'll have to forgive a few wobbly stanzas — but I think that you'll find —"

"I couldn't give a rat's conkers about your stupid bard!"
Hennic screamed at his sister as he clutched the bow
to his chest. "The only way you'll be getting Soulshot is
if I, and every last rabbit of Sparrowfast, dies first! I am
going to be the one to kill Scramashank. Agbert and
I will march out and destroy him. We don't need you,
your snotty children, or your ragged bunch of forest
robbers!"

Podkin suddenly found himself on his feet, with Paz
beside him. Most of Dark Hollow had jumped up too.
Fists were waved; teeth were gnashing. It looked as though
the council was about to turn into a brawl: Dark Hollow
against Sparrowfast. And in between were the Silverock
rabbits, their heads spinning with all this talk of Gifts and
Gorm, not knowing whom to side with, whether to be
excited or just plain terrified.

All eyes were now on Lady Enna: she stared at her
brother with such hatred that Podkin was surprised
his face didn't melt. She looked as though *she* was about
to throw the first punch when, instead, she took a deep
breath.

"Hennic," she said, "I'm not going to fight with you.
This isn't like the old days back home. You need to think
about my words and do what is best for every rabbit here,
not just for yourself."

She turned, looked across the longburrow at Podkin

and Paz, and then bowed her head. "Dark Hollow," she said, "we are leaving."

And then, without a word, all the Dark Hollow rabbits and the forest Wardens filed out of the longburrow, along the entrance tunnel and out of the warren to the patch of ground they had chosen to camp in. The wolves were already there, waiting for them.

—⁓—

As everyone began building campfires, Podkin watched them, thinking about the insults Hennic had thrown.

What was wrong with his uncle? Why hadn't he been impressed by the wolves and the Wardens? Podkin had been so sure, so *certain*, that the sight of his new friends would have convinced *anyone* to stand with them, even if it did mean handing over your tribe's Gift.

Riding out of the forest, wearing Blodcrun like some sort of horned king — had he been stupid to feel so proud? He felt a bit silly now, after Hennic's words, but then again . . . who else had managed to lead an army of wolves? Or discover the ancient secrets of the forest?

He tried to think of it from his uncle's point of view. Would he give up Starclaw if another Gift-Bearer came along? *If everything depended on it*, he thought, *if it was our only chance, then I would. I definitely would.*

So what, then, was Hennic's problem? Was it something to do with the Dark Hollow rabbits themselves?

A *ragged bunch of forest robbers*, he had called them. As if they'd been a gaggle of tinkers, turning up at his warren door uninvited.

They *were* a tatty lot, he supposed. They didn't have matching armor or any snazzy symbols painted on their shields. They were made up of all sorts: rabbits from warrens all over Gotland and Enderby. Every color of fur, every length of hair and shape of ears. Most of them were scarred or limping. Some appeared as though they hadn't eaten in months.

It *would* be easy to look down on them, Podkin thought. Especially if you came from a fine warren with mosaic floors and flags and tapestries everywhere.

But Podkin believed they had something no other tribe had.

They didn't judge one another by what they owned, or how they looked. Every rabbit was welcome at Dark Hollow, no questions asked. If you had lost your home, your family, your friends, then Podkin's new tribe would take you in. Take you in and fight for you, as if you were blood.

And, as ragged as they might be, they were the only ones who had managed to stand up to the Gorm so far.

They had courage and hope and a kind of wily resource-fulness that none of the old warrens possessed.

Sparrowfast and Silverock might *look* very impressive — lined up in rows with their shields, facing down the Gorm — but they probably wouldn't last two minutes. Not without Podkin's ragtag bunch to help them.

He couldn't help feeling a little tingle of pride.

No, Hennic's problem was elsewhere, he realized. It was all to do with his mother and what had happened between them when they were young. Whatever that was, his uncle had felt it so deeply and strongly that it blinded him even now. It had made him so angry that he would risk his own tribe — and everyone else's — just to spite Lady Enna, and Dark Hollow, and everything that went with her.

Podkin looked for his mother now and spotted her standing on the outskirts, gently rocking Pook back and forth. She hadn't spoken to anyone after her argument with Hennic, and she didn't look very happy, either.

He walked up to her and stood there for a few moments. Then, when she hadn't seemed to notice him, he gently put a paw on her arm.

"Podkin," she said, looking down at him over Pook's back, "darling, I'm afraid I'm too cross to talk right now. You understand, don't you? I just need a minute or two . . ."

Podkin could see damp fur around her eyes. The fight with Hennic had hurt her, too. The same deep hurt that drove his uncle. That went back years and years and years.

To get the bow, to stand the slightest chance against Scramashank, he would have to find some way to heal those old wounds. And how was he supposed to do that? *I'm only a child,* he thought. *Everyone expects me to tame wolves, fight monsters, discover ancient Gifts . . . and now sort out grownups' problems for them, when they can't even do it themselves. It's impossible.*

He remembered a little rabbit who used to spend the day hiding from his lessons, playing with his wooden wagon and model soldiers. What under earth had happened to *him?*

He became a hero, Podkin realized, and sighed. A *hero with another problem to solve.* There would be a way through this, somehow. Perhaps Brigid or Paz would have an idea. For now, he reckoned, it was best to leave his mother alone for a bit. To give her time to forget her sadness and go back to being the Lady Enna everyone was a little bit terrified of. The one he knew and loved.

"I understand." Podkin gave her arm a squeeze and moved away. He spotted Paz and Brigid setting up a cauldron to cook some soup and was about to go and ask their advice when he caught sight of Crom.

The big warrior rabbit had moved far away from

everyone else, over by the fences that encircled the rows and rows of little beehives. He was hunched over, as if in pain, and his arms were wrapped tightly around himself. Something was very wrong.

"What's the matter with Crom?" Rill, the black-furred shield-maiden, had walked up to Podkin and was following his gaze. She looked as worried as Pod.

"I don't know," Podkin said. "I think it's about something that was said in the meeting. When Hennic mentioned the witch-rabbit."

"How does Crom know about *her*?" Rill muttered under her breath, but Podkin still heard it.

"She was the one who took his sight," he said. "Didn't Crom ever tell you?"

Rill shook her head. "I didn't like to ask," she said. Then she set her jaw and grabbed Podkin's paw. "Come on." They began to march over to Crom.

As they drew closer, Podkin could see that the big rabbit's shoulders were shaking. Was he crying? Without thinking, Podkin pulled his paw away from Rill and ran up to Crom, throwing his arms around his waist. Crom froze for a moment, then knelt to return Podkin's hug, holding him tight for a long time.

Finally they let go, and Podkin stepped back to look into his friend's blank eyes. He saw fear there, and great sorrow, things he never thought Crom was capable of.

"What's the matter, Crom?" Podkin said. "Is it because of the witch?"

Crom nodded, then hung his head. "I never thought . . . I mean I hoped . . . that I'd never have to face her again. She was the last thing I ever saw . . . her face . . . the lightning . . . I still see it every night in my dreams. When Hennic said she was with the Gorm . . . I don't know what happened to me. I'm sorry, Podkin."

"Don't be sorry," Podkin said, hugging him again. "Don't ever be sorry."

Podkin knew exactly how he felt. He'd been the same with Scramashank for a long time after his father was killed. It was only after taking Surestrike, the hammer, from the Gorm leader that the terror had begun to go away.

"Crom," said Rill. She had been standing a few paces away, letting him have a moment with Podkin. "We need to talk. About the witch."

"What about her?" Crom said. He let Podkin go and sat down on the ground, leaning against the beehive fence. Rill and Podkin joined him.

"I know who she is," said Rill. "She came from Black-rock — my warren. I had no idea she was the one who took your sight . . ."

Crom gave a deep sigh, then nodded. "Tell me."

"Her name is, or was, Mila. She was our priestess, back before the Gorm came." Rill leaned her head back and looked up at the darkening sky, her voice sad and slow.

"She was young, for a priestess, but nice. At least, that's how I remember her. Our old priestess died suddenly — caught a chill one winter — and Mila was her apprentice. She still had a lot to learn, so the next spring, she went off to visit some warrens to the west. Toadleton, Muggy Pit, Sandywell. I think she was going to spend a few weeks in each. Learn some things from their priestesses.

"Anyway, what she learned was nothing good. She came back riding on a black-furred giant rat. A sleek, evil, nipping thing. And *she* had changed too. She wasn't nice anymore. She was so *angry* all the time. She shut herself away in the temple room and wouldn't let anyone in. Wouldn't perform any blessings or services. In fact, she refused to even mention the Goddess's name.

"Of course, we had no idea why at the time. We hadn't even heard of the Gorm then, although they must have been growing pretty strong inside that warren of theirs. All we knew was that Mila was different.

"It was when she started whispering things in the chieftain's ear that we got properly worried. My mother was friends with his wife, so she heard about it all. Mila was telling him to start digging downward, under the warren. She wanted him to tunnel out a deep pit, said there was lost treasure down there . . .

"Looking back, it's obvious she wanted us to dredge up some of that cursed iron you've told us about. Her mind had been turned by the Gorm, and they were using her to make our warren become like theirs.

"Luckily, Chief Rigel was having none of it. He even told her she wasn't wanted as a priestess anymore. So she left — that very night — but not before stealing our warren's Gift. Blixxen: the staff that can call lightning down from the sky.

"It was awful for Blackrock. Our Gift, the heart of the tribe . . . gone. But that wasn't the end of it. Mila came back a few months later, riding that cursed black rat of hers. This time she had Scramashank and a whole load of Gorm with her."

It was Rill's turn to cover her face and sob. "Not many of us survived," she managed to say. "Not my parents. Not my friends. And then there was the prison camp . . ."

There was silence among the three of them for a few minutes as they all thought back on what they had lost. Around them came the quiet buzzing of bees in their hives, the sound of campfires beginning to crackle.

"Thank you for telling me —" Crom began, when the peace of the evening was suddenly broken by a shout of alarm from the Dark Hollow camp.

"A crow!" someone screamed. "Up there! A Gorm crow!"

Podkin looked up, and there, sure enough, was the

outline of a jagged-feathered bird, flapping in lazy, clanking circles above their camp. It was one of the Gorm's spies: a crow, transformed into a rusty mass of blade-edged metal and cruel iron claws. It would be looking down on them with its empty red eyes, drinking in everything about them so that it could fly back and show its masters.

"A bow! Spears! Someone shoot it down!" Crom yelled beside Podkin, but the Dark Hollow rabbits had no bows, and the thing was too high for a spear to hit. All they could do was stand and stare back at the thing, willing it to fall out of the sky so they could get their paws on it.

Suddenly there was a zipping noise, and something shot up into the air, pinging hard against the metal body of the crow, causing it to flail and wobble. Its wings became gummed, covered in goo that was bringing it lower, lower, close enough for —

There was another *zip*, and a second missile shot up to hit the bird, this time causing a shower of sparks. The glowing flakes lit the goo that had been in the first missile, and instantly the crow was alight. It fell to the earth like a comet, flames streaking out behind it, and hit the ground with a *clang* that Podkin could feel through his feet.

A cheer went up, and Podkin took his eyes off the crow long enough to see the little forms of Mish and Mash. The two rabbits had arrived from Dark Hollow, a small group of new refugees behind them, and had been just in time to take down the Gorm spy with their blowpipe and slingshot.

They were running toward the downed bird now, daggers drawn, ready to finish it off.

Podkin almost cheered as well, but then he had a sudden, overpowering idea. *What if . . . ?* he thought, and then he was sprinting toward the crow himself, shouting, "Don't touch it! Don't kill it! I need it alive!"

Gormalech

When Podkin reached the crashed crow, all he could see was a mess of blackened metal shards poking out of a small crater in the ground. Flames still licked across the crow's body, and the thing was giving off a horrid stink of singed flesh and burning oil.

Podkin pulled off his cloak and threw it over the bird, kneeling to frantically pat it all over, trying to put out the flames.

"Hello, Podkin," said Mash, having arrived on the scene with his sister. "Why are you trying to save that horrible thing?"

The other Dark Hollow rabbits had begun to gather around, all of them wondering the same thing. Podkin ignored them and pulled the ruin of the crow out of the ground, wrapping it in his cloak so tightly it couldn't move. Its evil beak poked out of the top like a pair of twisted iron shears. Even though it was half his size, Podkin cradled it in his arms as if it were a baby. A very ugly, demon-possessed baby that would quite enjoy pecking his eyes out for its supper.

"Thank the Goddess," said Podkin. "I think it's still alive."

A single red eye glared out of the blanket, blinking with spite.

"You'd better have a good reason for this, Podkin," said Crom, his sword drawn, ready to stab into the enemy spy.

"Indeed," said Yarrow. "Make it something terribly exciting, would you?"

"The crown," Podkin said. "Where is it?"

He kept Starclaw, his dagger, and Moonfyre, the brooch, with him at all times, but as the crown was a lot bulkier, he had been storing it in his pack. Paz brought it over and unfastened the straps for him.

"Do you know what you're doing, Pod?" she asked, her voice so low that only he could hear.

"I think so." He looked up at her with worried eyes. The burning idea that had popped into his head now seemed a lot less clever. Verging on stupid, even.

She passed him the crown and he put it on, still

clutching the swaddled crow with his other arm. "Stand back, everyone," he said. He drew Starclaw, struggling to hold the dagger as it buzzed and jiggled with rage, and passed it to Paz. She held it for him while he touched a finger to the blade, instantly breaking the skin. A fat droplet of blood welled up on his fingertip. He moved it closer to the crow's beak.

"If anything goes wrong, Paz, I'll give you a signal. If you see me reach for Moonfyre, knock the crown off my head."

Paz nodded. The Dark Hollow rabbits stared on, wondering what he was going to try.

"Podkin, no!" Crom shouted, realizing what was about to happen, but it was too late. Pod's finger touched the crow's beak, his blood trickled into its mouth, and their minds touched.

Hunger.

That was the first thing Podkin felt.

A hunger so deep and so wide, it could literally swallow the whole world and everything in it, and still that wouldn't be enough.

Beneath that was rage.

Rage at being cheated, rage at being trapped beneath

the ground for *so* long. Away from all the tasty treats, all the things to swallow, to devour, to consume . . .

Podkin was like a tiny floating raft, dragged along a river into whirling rapids of frothing water. It was a long time before he could feel anything other than those two emotions; both were so strong, so totally *overpowering*.

At one point, he almost lost himself to it. He could feel himself leaking away, being dissolved into Podkin syrup and washed along in all the hatred. It took every inch of his willpower to hold himself together against the onslaught.

I *am Podkin*, he told himself. *Podkin, son of Lopkin, son of Bodkin. Podkin, brother of Paz and Pook. Friend of Crom and Brigid and Yarrow and Mish and Mash. I am the Gift-Bearer. I am the Moonstrider. I am the Wolf Rider.*

He repeated this over and over, wrapping himself around with his own identity, until he was sure he wasn't going to melt away.

All the time, he was hoping Paz would knock the crown off his head. He was hoping his mother would shout at him for being so stupid, that Crom would clonk him on the nose with the butt of his spear . . . He didn't care, just as long as he was out of the crow's mind.

And then he realized he had broken free from the torrent of emotion. Whatever he had done had worked, and now he was in the crow's thoughts but still separate.

Floating above, looking in, like someone gazing down at reflections in a pond. At the back of his head, as if in the distance, he could feel the minds of the three alpha wolves he had linked with. He shut them out as quickly as he could. They would not understand this. Podkin was not even sure if he would himself.

Below, he could see all the anger and greed that must be Gormalech. He could even see a tiny nutlike kernel that was the only part of the bird left. The god of living iron had totally overcome the creature, almost driving it out of its own being. This must be how he took over rabbits, too, Podkin realized. He forced them into a tiny ball of panic and then filled up what was left with himself. Did they understand what was happening? Was that little piece of crow struggling to break free and think for itself again?

Podkin held his breath, hoping and praying that the seething mind of Gormalech wouldn't spot him. Would he be able to look inside it without the thing noticing him? What would happen if it did? Would it take over his mind like it had the crow's? Would he become Gorm?

It was a deadly risk, but here was a chance — Podkin's only chance — to get a peek inside the iron armor of his enemy. He might be able to find out something important: a hint at how to beat them, a weakness, a flaw . . .

With his mind narrowed as small as he could make it, Podkin reached out and tried to see inside the raging mess that was Gormalech.

What are you? he thought, and somehow the idea was passed on, just like the images and scents that the wolves had shared with him.

He found Gormalech opening up, showing him the past, without seeming to realize what it was doing.

Glimpses and snatches were all Podkin had.

There were creatures: tall, earless things like the ones he had seen on carvings in the Ancients' tomb and the statues in Hern's Holt. These ones were moving and talking. Podkin couldn't understand what they were saying, but he had the sense that they were like parents to Gormalech. They were showing it things, teaching it. They were proud. Had they made it somehow? Was Gormalech one of their creations?

Then came scenes of caverns and tunnels under the earth. Gormalech was there, its liquid body flowing over and around everything. It was gathering and collecting, sucking up metals and oils and jewels from under the ground.

More glimpses of the Ancients came.

They were pleased with Gormalech, with the things it had found. It had brought them treasures from far beneath the surface, where they could not go, and doing their will made it happy. They had given it life somehow, with the sole purpose of plundering the earth for riches.

But something must have gone wrong. Next Podkin saw Gormalech dredging up more coal and ore, but instead of giving it back, it digested the stuff inside itself. It felt good to swallow things and make itself bigger. The more it ate, the better it felt, even though it knew it was doing wrong.

The Ancients were angry with their creation. Podkin saw them screaming at Gormalech, jabbing it with strange tools and weapons. He could sense Gormalech's fear and shame, but also that hunger again. It was too much to stop. It *had* to eat. It had to eat *everything.*

Some of the scenes that followed were too awful for Podkin to watch. The creature the Ancients had built turned upon its masters. It began to eat *them.* It swallowed their cities, their monuments. Running and screaming, they jumped in birdlike flying chariots and lumbering metal warrens that floated up from the ground. They fled into the sky, into the stars.

Now came loneliness along with the hunger. A deep loneliness mixed with shame, even as Gormalech continued to eat and eat and eat. It was angry with itself, angry with its masters for leaving it. The thing was a horrible, seething mass of bad, bad feelings.

The next part was missing—blanked out, Podkin

sensed—because suddenly Gormalech was trapped beneath the ground. This was the doing of Estra and Nixha, Podkin knew. The twin goddesses of life and death.

They had tricked Gormalech into a prison, and now its anger was directed at them. But there was nothing it could do, not for a long, long time. An age of lashing about in the darkness with only the sound of its metal body slithering against itself, while the temptation of things to be eaten up above drove it even more insane with rage.

And then something gazed in on it. Something new broke through the crust and peeped in. Podkin saw an image of a gray-furred being with an oversized copper helmet on its head. *Rabbit?* Gormalech thought. A *walking, talking rabbit?*

But it didn't matter what it was. Here was the thing it could use to break itself free, to overcome the goddesses. Podkin saw it take that first rabbit and twist it into a Gorm. Scramashank himself, he realized with a shudder, as the poor creature was stretched and torn into its new form.

And that copper helmet had power, just like Starclaw and the other Gifts. Gormalech bent that to its own will too. It poured its own essence into it, trying to create a weak point that it could use to shatter whatever kept it bound below.

Soon it would be on the surface again, and this time

it would eat it *all*. Even those secret things its masters had somehow locked away.

And there was nothing to stop it. Or almost nothing. Only one thing stood in its way. One tiny, laughable obstacle that could possibly hurt it.

Here Podkin saw a familiar image swim into view. The silhouette of three little rabbits, one of which had an ear missing... It was Paz, Pook, and himself, holding their Gifts in their paws. Except that the Gifts were like burning stars, giving off a powerful energy that burned and seared Gormalech. One Gift on its own it could cope with, but when several were brought together...

The more Gifts I get, the more it fears me, Podkin realized. He also began to see a chink in Gormalech's armor. It had put so much of itself into creating Scramashank, into taking over the power of the copper helmet... what would happen if that were suddenly destroyed?

Podkin mentally leaned forward, looking for a clue of some kind to back up his hunch. With all thoughts of hiding gone, he stared as hard as he could, opening himself up to being spotted.

As soon as he did it, he realized his mistake. He sensed Gormalech jolting into awareness, feeling itself being examined.

—*What?*

Podkin panicked. Back in his body, a million miles away, he could feel the crown begin to burn on his head. His chest burned as well, where Moonfyre was pinned. He tried to make his paw reach for the spot, but it was difficult to even feel his fingers. It was as if his body were a stuffed woolen toy, half a world away, and he was trying to move it using just his thoughts.

Finally, he was rewarded by the brooch's familiar zinging tingle through his paw, even as Gormalech spotted him, crouching as small as he could next to the speck of the crow's mind.

— You!

A tidal wave of anger began to build up, but before it could break, Podkin felt the crown being ripped from his head just as, in the same instant, the burnt crow itself died. The connection with Gormalech blinked out like a snuffed candle.

The real world came flooding back. He could feel the grass under his legs, smell the burning bird meat in his arms, and hear voices, lots of voices, screaming out his name.

Dropping the dead bird, he rolled to the ground, his little stomach clenching in shock. He felt himself being sick, over and over until there was nothing left, and then he collapsed to the ground and lay there, never wanting to move again.

—⁓—

"Here, drink this." Brigid was holding out a wooden cup of something that smelled of mint and chamomile. With a trembling paw, he took it and had a sip.

"What did you see?" Paz was kneeling beside him too, Blodcrun clutched in her lap. The rest of the Dark Hollow rabbits were gathered in a circle around them.

"I saw Gormalech," Podkin whispered. Everyone leaned in to hear him. "I saw inside its mind."

"Goddess save us," Brigid muttered, touching her heart, then her head.

"Did it ... see you?" Paz asked. Her eyes were wide, showing the whites all around.

"At the end. Maybe." Every rabbit there shuddered. "Paz, it's horrible. So hungry and empty. And so *angry*."

"What does it want?" Crom asked. "Is there a way to stop it?"

Podkin shook his head. "It's never going to stop," he said. "The Gorm are just a tool for it to break free of whatever the goddesses did to it. It's using them to get back up here because it wants ... it wants *everything*."

181

"What, gold?" Lady Enna asked. "Jewels? Land?"

Podkin looked at her with sad eyes. "No, Mother. *Everything*. It wants to eat the world. The Ancients. They made it to be hungry, but they got it wrong. It's nothing *but* hunger now. It can't stop, even though it wants to."

"I don't understand what he's talking about." Lady Enna spoke to Brigid, clearly worried that her son had lost his mind. "There must be something we can give it. Some way to stop it."

"There is one way," Podkin said. The rabbits leaned closer still. "Us," he said. "Pook and Paz and me. We're the only things it's afraid of. This is what I saw. If we use the Gifts, we can stop it. Only us."

"He's right," said Brigid. "I've known this all along."

"But how?" Paz asked. Even with all the Goddess's magic, they were still just children . . .

"Scramashank," said Podkin. "His helmet used to be a Gift. Changing it used up most of Gormalech's power. If we can destroy Scramashank . . . I think everything else might collapse."

If the Dark Hollow rabbits hadn't seen the truth of this already, they might have laughed. Three children destroy the Gorm Lord? But after all they'd been through together, it now made perfect sense.

"Well, that's not going to happen," said Enna. "Hennic is not going to let us have his bow. I know him better than anyone. Even after all these years, he hasn't changed. That stubborn, vain rabbit would rather his whole warren die than let a child of mine touch his precious Soulshot."

There was much murmuring and cursing among the Dark Hollow rabbits. So much that at first none of them heard Podkin speak.

"What did you say, Podkin?" Crom asked, his ears sharper than the others'.

"I said I can make him give it to us," Podkin repeated.

Lady Enna laughed bitterly. "No, you can't, Podkin. It doesn't matter that he's your uncle. There's not a rabbit in the Five Realms who could make that rat-witted idiot give us the bow."

"I've had an idea," said Podkin with a sigh. The solution had come to him as he sat looking at the body of the dead crow still wrapped in his smoldering cloak. It was yet another task he didn't want to do. Being a hero seemed to be all about doing things that anyone with half a brain would avoid. "Give me the crown, please, Paz."

Podkin got to his feet, still wobbling, and took Blodcrun from his sister. She stood too, and, leaning on her arm, Podkin headed back into Silverock Warren, explaining his plan along the way.

As they reentered the longburrow, they could see the council was still going. Hennic and Agbert were both on their feet, each trying to shout the other down.

"We can't wait for more tribes!" Hennic was yelling. "Two hundred Gorm is a lot, but it isn't *all* of them. We have to strike now, while we have even half a chance. If we don't, more reinforcements will arrive and everything will be lost."

Podkin hated to admit it, but his horrible uncle did have a point. They had to attack the Gorm as soon as possible, but only once Hennic had given up the bow.

"What do *you* want?" His uncle had stopped shouting and turned his head to watch Podkin and Paz limp up to the chieftain's table. "I thought you and your band of ruffians had taken the hint and left?"

"We're going," Podkin said, hoping his voice wasn't wavering too much. "But first I wanted to make peace between us."

"Yes," said Paz. "We didn't want to part on bad terms with you, Uncle. Perhaps we could drink a toast together?"

Hennic snorted and was about to say something nasty when he noticed that all the Silverock rabbits were staring at him. As much as it annoyed him, he needed them on his side if he stood a chance of driving the Gorm out of his warren.

"Very well," he said. He flicked his ears at a cupbearer, who brought two small drinking horns for Podkin and Paz. He set them on the table next to Hennic's silver tankard and filled them all with some golden mead.

Before Hennic could grab his drink, Podkin picked it up with both paws and held it out to his uncle, his eyes as big and innocent as he could make them. Hennic snatched the tankard from him with a grunt, too angry to notice that Podkin had dipped his cut finger over the lip and into the mead.

Hennic drained the drink, blood and all, and then slammed his tankard down on the table before Paz and Podkin had even taken a sip.

"Now," he said, "we've drunk. Hop along out of here so the proper chiefs can talk."

Podkin didn't move. Instead he drew Blodcrun out from under his cloak and placed it on his head. His uncle stared at him in outrage, green eyes flashing as if about to shout, and then his mouth suddenly went slack. All the rabbits in the longburrow gasped.

But Podkin didn't really hear them. His head was tingling, and he was experiencing that strange sensation of looking at himself through another pair of eyes again.

Except being in a rabbit's head was very different from being in a wolf or crow's. There were voices, thoughts, words, everywhere. A babble of overlapping chatter that was Hennic's mind talking to itself.

Podkin could feel his uncle's powerful pride. Pride for his warren, his bow, and his sparrows, but mostly a puffed-up sense of importance about himself.

There was a lot of anger, too. Hennic felt the world was a very unfair place. Why didn't he have more gold? More power? Why weren't other warrens begging for him to visit? What was so special about Silverock and their stupid mead? Applecross and their disgusting cider?

And there were some very deep and unpleasant feelings about his mother and her husband. Hatred wasn't a strong enough word for it. Uncle Hennic *loathed* Podkin's family, and here in his mind, Podkin could see that it all stemmed from the jealousy that divided them as children.

Why was Enna older than he? Why was she better at everything? How come she got to do everything first?

It made Podkin cringe. These were exactly the same feelings he used to have about Paz. In fact, he still did, sometimes. If it hadn't been for the Gorm and everything that had happened after, would he have ended up hating his big sister the way his uncle hated his? Would they have grown apart and turned into enemies?

But there wasn't time to worry about that now. Making

a silent promise never to resent his sister again, Podkin set about his task.

Remembering how he shared thoughts and memories with the wolves, Podkin reached out into his uncle's mind. He pushed past all the pride and bitterness, right into the core of Hennic's being. A spoiled little rabbit kitten was there: its paws curled around its precious things, terrified it wasn't really good enough to deserve them.

Stop being so childish, Podkin told it. *Stop whining and moaning, and take a look at* this.

There was a kind of floodgate in Podkin's mind. A door that blocked off all the worst feelings of terror and helplessness that the Gorm had aroused in him. Keeping it firmly shut was the best way he had found to deal with it, but now it all needed to come out.

Podkin opened it wide, kicked it off its hinges, and let everything pour into Hennic like an avalanche.

He showed him Scramashank standing off against Podkin's father. He showed him Lady Redwater and her Gorm crows; let him feel the pain of his ear being sliced off. He gave him the feelings of pure terror when he fought the Gorm in their camp, and when they fled from them at Boneroot. He let him smell the poisoned-iron stink of the metal pillar at Applecross as it took over the body of Comfrey, the priestess.

Next, Podkin called out to Truefang and the other alphas. He opened up his mind, joining them all with Hennic. Sensing what Podkin was doing, they added their own visions of the Gorm. The smell of the forest burning. The sound of trees being torn into matchwood.

Finally, Podkin pulled out his freshest memories: those he had just taken from Gormalech itself. Hennic got a firsthand taste of what that iron monster wanted to do to the world. That, and the fear it felt toward Podkin, Paz, Pook, and their Gifts.

We are the only ones who can stop it, Uncle. Podkin hammered the words home as if he were a blacksmith at an anvil. *But we can't do it without your bow. Soulshot doesn't belong to you. Not really. It was a Gift to your tribe, and to all rabbits. You must let us have it.*

Sensing he had done all he could, Podkin squeezed Paz's hand. She took Blodcrun from his head, breaking the link with Hennic. Podkin juddered, and blinked his eyes back into focus.

The whole of the longburrow was staring in silence. Hennic was still standing on the other side of the table, swaying slightly, his eyes glazed over as if he were sleepwalking. His mouth hung open, a small trickle of drool spilling from the corner.

He stayed like that for a long time: long enough for

Podkin to begin worrying he might have done some serious damage to his uncle.

Just as he was about to call for a healer, Hennic twitched. His ears jiggled and he blinked a few times, finally focusing on the little rabbit in front of him.

Podkin half expected him to start shouting again, or maybe even reach across the table and clout him around the ear. Instead, Hennic collapsed into his chair, his eyes filling up with tears.

Still silent, he reached down and brought out Soulshot, laying the beautifully carved bow on the table. He looked again at Podkin, stared deep into his eyes, and gave a single nod.

Then, with a trembling paw, he reached out and pushed the sacred Gift of his warren across the table to his nephew.

Interlude

Sythica clears her throat, making the bard pause in midflow.

"Yes?"

"I don't mean to interrupt," she says, "but it seems to be taking a long time to get to this battle . . ."

"It's coming," says the bard, trying not to sound too annoyed. "This is the buildup. You can't have an explosive final scene without a bit of buildup, you know."

"I see," says Sythica. She drums her fingers on the arm of her throne. "And I can't help remembering what you said earlier, about our order being part of the story?"

"It is," says the bard. He tilts his head. "A small part."

"So they'll be appearing in the battle, then." There is a

soft creaking sound as all the bonedancers lean forward together, eager for the answer.

"They might," says the bard. "Look. You can't just skip to different points when you feel like it. I'm trying to create an experience here. You have to go with the flow. Let the story take you with it, you know . . ."

"'Go with the flow,'" Sythica repeats. It's clearly an idea she isn't very familiar with.

The bard considers explaining further, then remembers he's on trial. A trial that could very well end up with him receiving a guided tour of a giant weasel's intestines. "The battle's coming up next," he says. "Right away. I promise."

A tiny clapping sound echoes around the hall as Rue applauds with excitement.

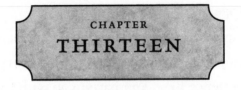

Battle

Podkin was surprised at how much effort went into getting ready for a battle. When he'd heard tales before, from traveling bards or one of his unfortunate tutors, he'd imagined the armies had just marched up, arranged themselves into lines, and gotten on with it.

Instead there had been hours and hours of talking and planning, late into the night. The Dark Hollow rabbits had been called back into the longburrow, and he and Paz found themselves right in the thick of everything, being consulted about each tiny detail.

Uncle Hennic, in contrast, had been almost silent throughout the whole affair. In fact, he looked as though he might take his rabbits and quick-march in the opposite direction. *Perhaps I did too good a job on him*, Podkin had thought.

Once everything had been decided, there was just enough time for a few hours' sleep, and then their army was on the march, heading for Sparrowfast and the biggest fight of their lives.

It had been agreed that Hennic's original plan was best. They had to strike at the Gorm before any more of them turned up. If they could manage to take care of Scramashank with the Gormkiller arrows, then it wouldn't matter how many Gorm there were. The battle would be over.

If Podkin's hunch was correct, that is.

There had been some talk of rabbits staying behind to look after the children, but everyone insisted on coming.

"Every spear will be needed," Lady Enna had said, surprising her children most of all. "If the Gorm beat our forces, they'll be upon *us* next and we won't survive anyway."

She didn't even object when Brigid suggested Podkin should be the one to fire Soulshot. But good old Uncle Hennic did.

"There's no way he can pull the bow. It's made for an adult, and a strong one at that."

Soulshot had been resting on the table before him.

Podkin plucked the string and hated to admit that his uncle was right. There was no way he'd be able to pull it far enough to shoot a daisy.

"How does it work?" he asked, hoping there was a magic trick to it.

"You draw and fire," said Hennic. Everyone in the longburrow glared at him as one, until he sighed, ears drooping. "All right. You shoot it with your body *and* your mind."

The assembled rabbits gave him a blank look. He sighed again and began to explain. "Usually, an archer stands before a target and aims. With Soulshot, you look at what you want to hit, and then *think* about it as well. Once you have the picture in your head, the bow will never miss. Wind, tired arms, bent arrows: it doesn't matter. A perfect shot, every time. You could aim at a target in the middle of a thunderstorm and still hit the center."

"And its weakness?" Podkin asked, thinking of the flaws all the other Gifts had.

"You have to focus completely on what you want to hit. If your concentration is broken, if you think of anything else by mistake . . ."

He didn't need to finish the sentence. There was silence for a few moments as the rabbits pondered what to do.

"Has anyone ever fired the bow with their eyes closed?" Crom asked.

Hennic thought for a moment, then nodded. "Yes. As

long as the target is in range. As long as you hold a picture of it in your mind. The arrow will still strike. Why?"

"Because if you don't need eyes to shoot it, then I can draw the bow," said Crom.

"I thought the one-eared child had to use it," said Hennic, through gritted teeth.

"Podkin can ride on my back. He can see for me. Once Scramashank is in our sights, I can picture him in my mind. I've smelled and heard him well enough to do that. The bow will do the rest."

Podkin couldn't help his breath catching a little at this idea. It would mean he'd be right in the thick of the fighting, for a start. He looked to Brigid and his mother for approval. They both nodded.

"That's settled, then," said Crom.

Podkin gulped. This was perhaps the most unpleasant task of all. But if Brigid thought he'd be all right . . . He looked to the witch-rabbit and was shocked to see tears in her eyes. Was something going to happen to him? Or to one of his family? Podkin moved to speak to her, but there was a sudden bustle as the tribal chiefs started placing wooden blocks on the longburrow table, mapping out the movements of their forces. Podkin was jostled this way and that, and when he found his balance again, Brigid was gone.

And so the rabbits were all given places. Warriors at

the front, everyone who could hold a spear or bow at the back. The wolves on one flank, the Wardens on the other. All would fight for as long as they could, for as long as it took for Crom and Podkin to shoot down Scramashank. The rest was in the paws of the Goddess.

—⁓—

At daybreak, they set off.

They made a very strange procession: all the rabbits of Silverock, Sparrowfast, and Dark Hollow, accompanied by the giant Wardens and a huge pack of wolves.

They headed to the Razorback Downs, then turned west, keeping to the steep banks of the hills. When they faced their enemy, they wanted the advantage of the high ground.

Finally, when they were halfway to Sparrowfast Warren, a small bird came fluttering out of the sky and onto Hennic's outstretched paw. He took the tiny scroll of parchment from its leg and read the message aloud.

"The Gorm know we are coming. They are marching out of my warren to meet us."

"How many?" Crom asked. "Where are they coming from?"

Hennic shrugged and scowled. "That's all it says. The message scroll is tiny."

"Can you send another back?" Lady Enna asked. "Can you ask for more details?"

"I can try," said Hennic. His hatred for his sister seemed to have been overtaken by his newfound fear of the Gorm. "Although it's likely my scout is dead already."

"No time," said Mo Grim, who had walked over to see what they were talking about. "The enemy approaches."

The Warden pointed a finger toward the horizon, where a gray smudge could be seen.

The Gorm army, marching steadily toward them.

"Shield wall!" Crom's voice was loud enough for the whole company to hear. The trained warriors were quick and efficient. Silverock and Sparrowfast, followed by Dark Hollow, formed into two lines, one behind the other, then locked their shields into formation, poking their spears through the gaps. From the front, all that could be seen was a long wooden wall colored in bands — silver, sky blue, and black — and painted all over with bees, sparrows, and pinecones.

The Wardens lumbered over to their side, lining up with their staffs ready: eight fearsome giant rabbits filled with the rage of the forest (Pocka having been left behind the wall with the archers).

Podkin, sitting atop Crom's back just behind the Dark Hollow shields, put Blodcrun on his head again. He used it to call to the wolf alphas, signaling where they should gather with their packs. Through them, he could smell the iron stink of the Gorm already, wafting toward them in a stinging, invisible cloud. The wolves wanted to rush toward it and attack immediately. Podkin had to show them over and over again where he wanted them to go, filling his thoughts with pleas and desperation, until finally they gathered on the right flank with much snapping of teeth and growling.

Through it all, Podkin could sense his uncle's mind, lingering at the edge of his thoughts, full of fear and resentment. At least the link to Gormalech had completely broken when the crow died. Just thinking about it made Podkin shudder. He took the crown off his head as soon as he could and stowed it in his backpack.

He wished there was time to speak to Brigid about her tears, and to give his mother and Paz a final hug, but everything was happening so quickly.

Behind the warriors, the rest of the warrens gathered themselves in a loose formation high up on the banks of the downs. Bows, arrows, and spears were given out. Some had slings and stones, and Mish and Mash had their blowpipe and slingshot ready. They stood next to Paz, who was being given a final lesson by Brigid on how to use the sickle. Yarrow had Pook on his back; Lady Enna was holding a longbow, one arrow already nocked. Even Pocka had a spear. All were ready to fight for their lives.

And so they stood, watching the gray smudge on the horizon get closer and closer until they could see the spiked, twisted metal forms of the Gorm themselves.

—⁓—

The sound of their marching was like thunder. Two hundred suits of thick iron plating, rasping and grinding as they stomped onward.

The ground shook. The air around them pulsed with the stink of hot metal and dark, poisonous energy. Podkin didn't need the borrowed senses of the wolves to smell and feel it. His fur bristled all over, his ear flattened to his head. He felt the urge to run, or thump the ground in alarm, and recognized the old instincts of his species. He wondered if the other rabbits around him felt the same.

"Podkin." Crom turned his head to call up to him. "What's that screeching, churning noise?"

It's the Gorm army, turnip-head! Podkin felt like shouting, then realized that Crom's sensitive hearing must be picking out something else. He looked at the approaching enemy again and saw something hideous behind them: five of the forest-eating machines, rolling steadily onward with those slave-filled wheels.

"The machines," he told Crom. "The things that were tearing up the forest."

"Hern's antlers," Crom cursed. He and Podkin were clearly thinking the same thing. If those constructions could rip through a forest of iron-strong oak, what would they do to rabbit flesh and bone?

Still the Gorm army ground on. Closer and closer, until Podkin could make out the spikes and shards of their armor.

The frontline was made up of riders on giant armored rats. Infantry came next, with spears and halberds hung with rabbit skulls and chopped-off ears. Behind were the wheeled machines, being whipped on by slave masters, and up above circled a flock of iron-feathered crows.

They marched until they were fifty feet away, then stopped.

Up on the banks, all the rabbits in each tribe held their breath, tightened their grip on their weapons. Podkin could hear a low rumbling as all sixty wolves started growling deep in their throats.

The only other sound was the flapping and clanking of the Gorm crows as they circled overhead.

And then the Gorm ranks parted. Something was coming through.

"Scramashank," was all Podkin could say.

Crom turned sideways, into an archer's stance. He raised Soulshot, drawing the string back to his ear. The bow creaked. Podkin could feel the thick muscles in Crom's shoulders tense.

"If we can hit him now, this might all be over," Crom said, his jaw clenched with the effort of holding the bow.

"Hang on," said Podkin. "I can't see him yet."

He stared at the Gorm ranks. Through the gap came a giant rat, then another. The first was black-furred, ridden by a robed rabbit with a spiked iron crown. She didn't look like any Gorm Podkin had ever seen, but clutched in one paw was a long, jagged staff. Crackles of electricity played along its length, ready to call lightning from the sky to blow holes in the defense of the shield wall.

"Mila. The witch," Podkin whispered. At the mention of her name, he felt Crom tense even more.

The second rider followed, emerging from the ranks to stand next to Mila. This one Podkin knew well. His rat was bigger than the others, his armor more warped and spiked, his helm topped off with mismatched horns.

"I see him!" Podkin almost shouted in Crom's ear. "It's Scramashank!"

The Gorm leader was sitting high in his stirrups, his arms spread wide, gesturing at the force opposing him and laughing in mockery. His Gorm warriors were laughing too, waving their swords and spears in a show intended to terrify the tribes.

"What is this I see before me?" Scramashank bellowed. "Is this the best that—"

"Now, Crom!" Podkin shouted, slapping the big warrior on his shoulder.

Crom pointed the bow toward Scramashank's voice and let fly the first Gormkiller arrow.

It *swished* from the bow, a bolt of shining bronze. Podkin tracked it as it flew over the heads of the Dark Hollow warriors, crossed the space between the two armies in half a heartbeat, heading straight for Scramashank . . .

. . . and then *swerved* in the air at the last instant, bending to the left and smashing into Mila the witch's lightning staff.

There was a sound like a thunderclap. A wave of invisible force burst out from the destroyed staff, knocking one or two Gorm to their feet. Podkin felt a sharp buzz of energy from Starclaw and Moonfyre at the same time. Something had happened to the Balance of power.

"Did I hit him?" Crom asked.

"No!" Podkin shouted. "You hit the witch's staff! Fire again!"

There was shock in the Gorm lines. Scramashank was staring at the witch beside him. She was clutching her hand, screaming. Neither of them realized what had just happened.

Crom grabbed a second Gormkiller arrow, nocked it, drew, and loosed.

"Scramashank! Think of Scramashank!" Podkin yelled, but it was too late. The second arrow followed the first, heading for the Gorm Lord, then turning at the last moment. This time it hit the witch herself, knocking her clean off the back of her rat.

You shoot it with your body and *your mind*, Hennic had said. Crom's thoughts were filled with hatred and fear of the witch, Podkin realized. He couldn't concentrate on anything else. The bow had seen Mila standing next to Scramashank and thought *she* was the target.

"You hit the witch again!" Podkin looked down to see only one Gormkiller remained. If Crom missed with that one too, all was lost.

"I can't help it!" Crom shouted back to him. "What shall we do, Podkin?"

But there was no time to decide. The Gorm had recovered from their shock. Mounted guards rushed forward to shield Scramashank, and then the Gorm Lord's voice could be heard again, screaming in rage this time.

"Charge! Charge! Destroy them!"

There was an echoing clank as all the Gorm leveled their weapons, and then the Gorm were upon them.

⌁

Podkin wanted to shout "Here they come!" but all that came out was "Hyaaaaa!"

All those bards with their stories of epic battles and heroic deeds had lied to him. This wasn't exciting or noble or adventurous — this was just plain terrifying.

There was a wild wave of snarling and howling from his right as the wolves leaped forward, hurling themselves toward the charging Gorm. They met half of the oncoming enemy in the middle of the battlefield with a crash that threw wolf and Gorm bodies up into the air.

The rest of the Gorm army continued, storming toward them like a surging wave of iron.

"Fire!" A yell that sounded like Paz. Spears, arrows, and stones flew over Podkin's head, pinging off the charging Gorm like a mildly annoying hailstorm. On they came, regardless.

"Brace yourselves!" came a cry from someone, and Podkin saw the warriors behind their shields lean into the wall of wood. A wall that now looked incredibly flimsy.

An instant later, the Gorm crashed into it. There was a crunch of timber; splinters flew; spears snapped. For a brief moment the wall held, but then rabbits fell in two, three places. Spiked, armored Gorm soldiers burst through the gaps, swinging swords, clubs, and halberds.

And then ... chaos.

Gorm were everywhere. Soldiers tried to hold them back, to find chinks in their armor, but there were none. They shrugged off the copper and bronze blades of the tribes, knocking brave rabbits to the ground.

Wolves dashed in all directions. They leaped at the Gorm, bearing them down, but even their saber-toothed fangs weren't strong enough to pierce the iron armor. Podkin saw a few managing to tear off helmets to get at the flesh beneath, but most were pushed or knocked away, falling to Gorm spears and swords.

From Crom's back, Podkin looked around frantically, trying to spot Scramashank. But the Gorm leader had learned his lesson. He must have dismounted and hidden himself among his troops. Try as he might, Podkin couldn't spot those telltale lopsided horns.

Would Soulshot work if Crom just fired anywhere? Would the arrow somehow find its way to its target in all this confusion? *As long as the target is in range,* Hennic had said. Did that mean just within firing distance, or in actual sight of the bow?

Perhaps if they'd had a spare arrow they could try, but there was only one left. There could be no risk involved now. Podkin had to be *absolutely* sure he had a clear shot. If they missed with the last arrow . . . *everything* was lost.

The Gorm were pressing into them, pushing them back up the hill.

One came close to Crom, who lashed out with Soulshot, catching it across the creature's metal face. The touch of the magic bow drove it back, screaming, and Podkin had a few more seconds to try to spot his target.

He saw the Wardens sweeping left and right with their staffs. Clouds of insects swept over the Gorm; spiders crawled through cracks in their armor, biting with tiny poisoned fangs. Of all the tribes' forces, they seemed to be doing the best, but even they were overwhelmed.

Podkin looked back to where Paz and the others were still sending spears and arrows, as useless as they were, into the Gorm.

He saw his mother, Mish, and Mash shooting over and over again, knocking swooping iron crows out of the sky.

Paz was with Brigid, holding up the sickle and trying to do some kind of magic. To his horror, Podkin saw a Gorm soldier break through the line of warrior tribesmen and charge at his sister.

In slow motion he saw the creature raise its sword, swinging it back for a fatal blow. Paz had her eyes shut, focusing on her spell, unable to move out of the way.

Before Podkin could even scream, Brigid stepped calmly in front of his sister, blocking the path of the blade. The Gorm stumbled, its sword arm clutched tight by the old witch-rabbit, its helmet pelted by smoking, blazing bullets from Mish and Mash.

Podkin saw the thing fall, covered by rabbits with spears, pulling off its armor and stabbing at the body beneath.

Paz was still there, eyes open now, screaming at something.

Brigid was nowhere to be seen.

"Podkin! Where is he, Podkin?"

Crom's yells drew Pod back to the battle. Still no sign of Scramashank: just a sea of spiked metal bodies crashing into them in endless waves. Behind the Gorm troops were the clanking, grinding death machines — only a few minutes away from chewing the rabbit army to pieces.

"I can't see him!" Podkin yelled. "I can't see him anywhere!" *Goddess, help me,* he prayed. *Father, help me.*

The Gorm were all over them, unstoppable, merciless. Around him, rabbits and wolves were falling like stalks of wheat under a scythe. He felt Starclaw buzzing at his side, but he knew the dagger was useless against this enemy. Moonfyre was useless; Blodcrun was useless. Without a target, Soulshot was useless.

Beside him, among the toppling remains of the Sparrowfast rabbits, Podkin caught sight of his uncle, sitting on his giant rat and yelling at his troops.

"Fall back! Sparrowfast, fall back!" Hennic yelled. "All is lost! All is lost!"

None of his men could hear him over the deafening clangs of copper against iron, iron against shield and flesh, but Podkin did.

He heard him, and with a sickening dread, he realized Hennic was right.

The Final Blow

On and on they came.

"Move back, Crom!" Podkin shouted. "Back, back!"

Crom turned and ran up the hill, Podkin clinging to his neck. The tribes' frontline was now in tatters. The machines had reached the fighting, and rabbits, wolves, and Gorm were all trying to avoid their whirling, chopping blades.

"Podkin! What's happening?" Crom came to a halt next to Pod's mother. She was still firing arrows, trying to hit as many of the Gorm crows as she could. The things were swooping down, slashing and pecking at the fighting rabbits' heads before flapping off to circle again.

"We missed Scramashank," Podkin called to her over the noise of battle. "We hit the witch instead."

"Why aren't you shooting again?"

"I can't see him! We've only got one arrow left!" Podkin looked down to where Paz was clutching her sickle. Tears were streaming down her face. "Paz! Are you all right?"

"Brigid..." was all Paz could say. She pointed to the fallen Gorm, beneath which a scrap of Brigid's cloak poked out.

Podkin gulped. He felt his blood run cold, felt his heart lurch in his chest. There was no way Brigid could have survived, but still... he wanted to leap from Crom's back right then and pull her out, help her if he could. There might be a chance she wasn't... But he knew if he spent even a minute doing that, they were doomed. *Find Scramashank. Shoot the arrow,* he told himself. *Then you can go to Brigid.*

"Paz!" he shouted. "You have to focus. We need the power of the sickle. The battle is nearly over — we're going to lose!"

"Podkin's right," said Crom. "There's no time for this now. Use what Brigid taught you. See if you can clear a path to Scramashank for us."

"Yes. Right." Podkin watched as Paz took a deep breath, closed her eyes, and began to focus again. He felt a rush of pride for his sister, then turned his eyes back to the fighting. Scramashank was still nowhere to be seen. Had the Goddess forsaken them? Was it really going to end like this?

"Zah! Zah!" from somewhere behind him he heard Pook shout. Yarrow was trying to keep him quiet, but the little rabbit wouldn't stop. "Zah! Zah!"

Finally, Podkin spun around. "Pook! Paz is trying to concentrate! You need to be quiet!"

Pook was pointing up to the top of the downs with a chubby finger, his face beaming with excitement. Podkin followed his gaze and saw something that made his heart leap.

All along the ridge of the downs were rabbits, black robed, with masks of bone. Pook had been calling out "Zarza," the name of the bonedancer assassin they had befriended on their mission to find Surestrike. But there wasn't just one Zarza. There was an army of them.

"Bonedancers!" Podkin shouted. "The bonedancers are here!"

As if his yell had summoned them, the dancers began to spill down the sides of the downs, rushing into the battle like flowing ink. Their black-and-gray robes billowed out behind them. They leaped and twirled in somersaults, eyes flashing behind their masks of bone.

A cheer went up from the battered tribes as they

watched the bonedancers sweep into the Gorm. Up, over, and around they spilled, lashing out with their curved swords and sending showers of darts into the tiniest of gaps in the Gorm armor.

For the first time in the battle, the Gorm began to fall back. It filled the tribes of rabbits with new energy. They pulled together, slamming up shield walls and trying to push forward themselves.

"Well met, earless one." Podkin looked away from the fighting to see a bonedancer standing before him. From the gray eyes and patterns on her mask, he recognized Zarza, his friend.

"Zarza!" Podkin had never felt happier to see someone in his life. "How did you know we needed you?"

"Later," she said. "Now I must fight. I leave my sister here to keep you safe."

She beckoned a second bonedancer over, this one wearing white robes and, surprisingly, no mask. She was a young, white-furred rabbit with blue eyes and a heart-shaped patch of gray fur on her nose.

"This is Syrena. She is a novice. Her mask is yet to be earned." Zarza clasped wrists with her sister before bowing to the rest of them. "Die well."

Then she turned and somersaulted into the fray, lost in the mass of fighting, clashing bodies.

"I'd really rather not die at all," Yarrow began to say, but was interrupted by a piercing shriek. Three Gorm crows swooped down from the sky, metal beaks open and talons grasping.

Syrena spun to meet them, cutting one from the air with her curved bronze sword. The other two dodged: one headed for Yarrow and Pook, and the third swerved around Syrena's blade, doubling back to hook its claws into her neck. Syrena screamed, reaching up to strike at the thing as it pecked with its beak, aiming for her eyes and throat.

"Take that!" Yarrow shouted, bringing his spear up just in time for the crow to impale itself on it. Pook fell to the ground in the scuffle.

Podkin looked across to where Syrena was struggling with the bird. Could he get Crom to shoot it off with Soulshot? But then their last arrow would be gone. What if his mother shot with her bow? She might hit Syrena . . .

Just as he was panicking over what to do, there was a *ping* as something whacked into the crow's metal body. *Ping! Ping! Ping!* Little rocks were flying at the bird, making it lose focus. Podkin looked down and saw Pook, a grim expression on his chubby face, hurling the carved bones Brigid had given him. *Ping! Ping! Ping!*

The crow turned its head to scream at Pook. It was enough for Syrena to get a grip on the bird's neck. With a wrench and a twist, she threw the broken thing to the ground. She was bleeding from several scratches, but none were serious. Pook had saved her eyesight, maybe her life.

She reached down and picked up one of his carved bones, held it up to him, and nodded her thanks before tucking it into her robes and readying her sword. More Gorm were coming.

Podkin turned his attention back to the battle. With bonedancers, wolves, and forest Wardens, the tribes seemed to be holding their own for a moment, but it wouldn't last long. The Gorm machines were moving steadily forward, heading toward the reassembled shield walls of Dark Hollow and Sparrowfast. If they hit them, everything would be over.

But where was Scramashank? With the scores of fighting bodies everywhere, it was impossible to see. He needed something to clear the way, just for a moment.

"Paz? Are you going to do something with Ailfew?" he called to his sister, thinking her magic could be their only chance.

"Soon," was all she said. Her eyes were still closed, her jaw clenched. Podkin imagined she must be calling on the roots and plants below the downs to grow up, like she had on Ancients' Island. But what was taking her so long?

Then he felt it. Not the growth of thorns and tendrils, but a fresh breeze, blowing across them from the downs. Soft at first, but building steadily, picking up seeds and pollen and dew, turning into a rolling mist that billowed down into the battlefield.

This must have been what Brigid was showing her at the start of the battle. A mist filled with the Goddess's power, just like the one Brigid called when they rescued their mother from the Gorm camp.

Podkin remembered how it had affected the enemy then, making them writhe and scream. This time it was even more powerful.

The mist was the breath of the downs themselves. It was filled with the scent of clover and buttercups, the breath of ants and beetles, the essence of the bedrock itself and all the billions of tiny prehistoric creatures that had formed it. It was timeless and potent. To Podkin, it smelled of long summer afternoons spent basking in the lazy sun. To the Gorm, it was like poison gas: choking, burning, stinging.

The armored warriors stopped fighting to clutch at their throats and their eyes, roaring with pain. Some of them fell to their knees or rolled on the ground, suddenly opening up Podkin's view.

This was his chance.

He sat up high on Crom's back, eyes flicking over the toppling Gorm, trying to spot his quarry. There, by the machines? No, just another choking soldier. There, wrestling with those wolves? No again.

And then, just when it seemed Scramashank had vanished from existence, Podkin saw him.

He was standing in a circle of fallen Gorm. While his bodyguard had been overpowered by the mist, Scramashank was still upright, clamping his hands over his mouth. Podkin knew him instantly: those mismatched iron horns, that foot of twisted, jagged iron . . . they had him.

"I see him, Crom!" Podkin shouted. "Draw now! NOW!"

Soulshot creaked as Crom heaved the string back to his ear. Podkin watched him take a moment to focus, imagining Scramashank in his mind. But would that be enough? He had heard him, smelled him, as he had said. What if Soulshot needed more?

Quickly, Podkin summoned up every memory he had. Scramashank drawing his sword to kill his father, Scramashank at the battle of Boneroot, at the camp where Podkin cut off his foot. He remembered his voice, his flashing eyes, the evil sneer he gave every time he thought he was going to beat Podkin.

All those memories, all that terror he had felt and overcome — Podkin let it flood through him until he felt his little paws tremble with emotion. And then, when he almost couldn't take any more, he reached out a finger and touched the taught bowstring.

In that moment of contact, he *felt* the bow leap to

attention as if it had been waiting for him all along. Suddenly it knew its target. It had a purpose. It sang a buzzing song of joy, and Podkin could feel Starclaw and Moonfyre joining in, their power coursing through him like lightning through a copper rod.

He leaned down to whisper in Crom's ear.

"Now."

There was a *thrum* as Crom loosed the arrow.

Podkin watched it fly, a bronzed, sparkling streak, filled with the magic of his Gifts.

It swooped low over the heads of the rabbits, jinking left and right with a life of its own.

Scramashank was still standing among his fallen warriors, screaming at them to get up. His flashing red eyes flicked over the battlefield as if he knew what danger he was in.

As Podkin watched, he saw Scramashank catch sight of him up on the hill. The Gorm Lord's eyes took in Crom, the empty bow, the look of hopeful glee on Podkin's face.

And then he saw the flash of bronze heading straight for him.

Podkin thought he saw Scramashank mouth the word "No," but he couldn't be sure. The Gormkiller arrow was on him too quickly. It smashed into the center of his twisted helmet — the thing that used to be the sacred Gift of Sandywell Warren — and exploded.

Podkin saw the helmet fly apart, revealing—for an instant—the scarred, burnt face of the rabbit underneath. Then that flew apart too, with a wall of force that knocked every rabbit on the battlefield to its feet. Crom toppled backwards, taking Podkin with him, and as they fell, Podkin felt twin electric shocks from Moonfyre and Starclaw, like little bolts of lightning on his skin.

He found himself on the ground, pinned under Crom's head, but looked up in time to see the Gorm machines topple, crumbling into pieces as they fell. The Gorm themselves, already writhing on the field, screamed louder than ever. Their iron armor crumbled and flaked, peeling off in withered strips.

And somewhere beneath the earth, Podkin was sure he heard a matching scream: one of rage and frustration and pain. Gormalech had put all his power into one gamble, and he had been beaten by the Goddess again.

After that, everything was quiet.

CHAPTER FIFTEEN

Afterward

———

Podkin stood alone on the battlefield.

It was morning again. All the other rabbits were still asleep in Sparrowfast Warren, where they had spent the night.

They had gone there when the battle was through, Hennic and his tribe overjoyed to be home and free from the Gorm. There had been cheering and tears of relief, but Podkin and his friends were too numb to join in.

Sparrowfast was a beautiful warren, with a ring of wooden aviaries around the mound and delicate tapestries of birds in flight everywhere. The Gorm had splintered a few doors but hadn't been there long enough to do too much damage.

Not that Podkin had noticed. He and Paz had found an

empty room and collapsed on the bed, too exhausted and shocked to even cry.

Brigid. Gone.

With Crom's help, they had moved the dead Gorm soldier and his broken armor to find their friend underneath.

Brigid, who had found them in the woods and saved them from the Gorm. Brigid, who had helped them rescue their mother and had nursed her back to health. Who had guided them and helped them every step of the way, always with a kind word and a twinkle in her eye.

She'd been their mother when they needed one. She'd been their friend, their teacher, their guardian.

She looks so small, Podkin had thought, half expecting her to open an eye and make a comment about how she'd known this was going to happen and had dodged the Gorm blade at the last minute. *Had* she known? And if so, why hadn't she moved? Why hadn't she brought a shield with her? Some armor?

It was my time, Podkin. That's just the way things had to be. He heard her voice in his head so clearly, for a second he thought she'd spoken.

"Wake up. Wake *up*," Paz had said, taking hold of her paw. Podkin took the other. It was cold, limp, lifeless.

"She's gone," Crom had said, his voice as soft as Podkin had ever heard it. Looking up, Podkin had seen tears welling in the blind warrior's eyes. "She's in the Land Beyond. She's there with her family. Looking down on us right now. She'd be so happy that we won. So proud of you both."

"No." Podkin had only been able to whisper that word. A whisper, when what he wanted to do was *shout*. He wanted to scream at the Goddess how it wasn't fair, how Brigid had only ever served her, how she didn't deserve to be lying dead on a battlefield, covered in Gorm blood.

"Come on, son," Crom had said. He had gently taken Brigid's paws back and laid them on her chest before wrapping her in her cloak and lifting her from the ground. She was as light as a twig in Crom's arms. "Let's take her home."

They had brought her into the Sparrowfast longburrow and laid her before the fire, where all the Dark Hollow rabbits gathered to weep over her, holding one another tight in their sorrow.

And she wasn't the only one to have died: Clary, the soldier from Munbury Warren; Dodge, the councilor. Rabbits from Sparrowfast and Silverock, and some of the Dark Hollow warriors Podkin hadn't even met properly yet. Wolves too: brown, black, and gray puddles of fur lay motionless on the field among all the fragments of crumbling iron.

The Wardens had all survived, thankfully, but some

were hurt. Cob and Vendra, in particular, had nasty spear wounds. They would have to go back to the Grimwode quickly to heal.

And there were many Gorm.

Peeled of their iron shells, they just looked like ordinary rabbits. Well, perhaps not quite ordinary. Their fur was seared off in patches. Black veins bubbled all over them, and some had splinters and scabs of metal growing through their skin.

Many had died the instant Scramashank's helmet exploded. Others were still breathing—shallow, pained breaths—or even trying to crawl weakly away. The tribes left them there, for the time being. Nobody wanted to put their paws on the Gorm or their cursed metal.

They left that job until the evening, so Podkin heard. Rabbits from all three tribes had returned to the battlefield to build a funeral pyre. When they got there, they found fewer Gorm bodies than they had expected. Maybe some *had* managed to drag themselves off somewhere. Maybe Gormalech himself had reached up through the earth to pull them back down. Would they still be Gorm without their armor? Or would their own minds manage to reclaim their bodies? Podkin found he couldn't bring himself to care. Not now. He couldn't feel anything except a terrible sadness.

The towering funeral pyre stood on the field among the fragments of armor that still lay everywhere, a mountain of bodies, wood, and leaves. They would burn it tonight and stand to watch the smoke rise up over the downs. And then tomorrow they would go home: back to their proper lives, without having to live in terror anymore.

Podkin couldn't even imagine what that would be like. Fear of the Gorm had become a part of him over the past months. It was as natural as breathing. Could it really be finished? Was he really able to be a normal rabbit again?

His thoughts were interrupted by a distant howl. He looked up to see Truefang, Nightclaw, and Deadeye with their packs gathered around them. They were hovering on the edge of the battlefield, keen to be back in the cool darkness of the forest.

Podkin thought of putting on Blodcrun and asking them to stay for the funeral ceremony, but what would wolves understand about that? Their brothers and sisters were gone; they were left. That was all. That, and the fact that the forest was now safe.

Podkin was surprised they had stayed around *this* long. He raised a paw in farewell and watched them turn as one and lope back to Grimheart.

Alone again, Pod began to wander among the scraps and shards of metal. Here and there was a puddle of dried blood, buzzing with little flies. He walked past cracked helms, crumbling shoulder plates, shattered fragments of swords and daggers.

They had already found what was left of Mila the witch's lightning staff. It was just a twisted copper stick now, blackened and burnt. Podkin had offered it to Rill, as it was once the Gift of her warren, but she refused. It was now in his pack, next to Blodcrun. Two more Gifts for his collection. Now he had six. Half the Gifts that the Goddess had given. *Is there any point to having them now?* he wondered. *Why am I even out here looking for more?*

He didn't know. It just felt like something he should do.

Podkin brushed his toes through the grass, turning over the bits and pieces of iron. Some of them crumbled into dust as he nudged them.

He walked past the heaps of wood and metal that had been the fearsome tree-tearing machines. The tribes had managed to free the slaves after the battle. The poor, half-starved rabbits were now in the Sparrowfast longburrow, being treated with the rest of the wounded.

All except one. The pyre builders had found another body inside one of the broken wheels. That of a scrawny, ginger-furred rabbit with burnt and blistered skin around his neck.

Vetch.

The traitor had run back to his masters and been rewarded by getting shoved into a treadmill. The hard work had killed him — either that or the shock of the explosion. Podkin probably should have felt happy that he got what he deserved, but he didn't. It just added to the weight of sadness already pulling him down. What a waste of a life. And all for the sake of a bit more gold.

Podkin looked up at the pyre where Vetch now lay, along with Brigid and the others. He hoped things would be better for them all, wherever they were headed next.

Just as he said his little prayer, his foot bumped against something solid. There in the grass, resting on his toe, was a chunk of copper. The edges were blackened and jagged, but Podkin could make out a bit of rim left at the bottom, as if it had once been part of a pot or bowl. He bent to look closer and noticed two more pieces nearby. He felt Starclaw give a little buzz, and underneath their coating of soot, the copper pieces twinkled in response.

Carefully, Podkin gathered them up and held them in his paws.

"Are you ... were you ... the Gift of Sandywell?" he said, mainly to himself. He thought the shards might have glimmered again in answer, although it was probably just the sun peeping behind a cloud and bouncing off the metal.

Podkin scanned the ground again, looking for more fragments or some trace of the Gorm Lord. Some of the skulls from his belt, his black iron sword . . . anything. But there was nothing left except a circle of flattened grass.

———⁓———

That night, the rabbits of Dark Hollow, Silverock, and Sparrowfast all gathered on the field again, this time in a ring around the pyre.

Chief Hennic came forward with a blazing torch. Podkin thought he might say something pompous — try to take credit for the victory, perhaps — but he just bowed his head and lit the wood.

Paz clutched Podkin's hand on one side, Crom took his hand on the other. Pook was cuddled up in his mother's arms, with Yarrow beside her. Mish and Mash were there, and Zarza and Mo Grim. Everyone who had been a part of Podkin's life since the Gorm invaded his warren.

They all watched the flames lick up the sides of the

pyre, turning it into a pyramid of blazing orange light. Smoke and showers of glowing sparks poured up and up, blowing over the downs and on into the sky.

As the pyre began to burn down, some rabbits turned and headed back to Sparrowfast Warren for the night's feast. But Podkin and his friends stayed until the very last log had collapsed and there was nothing but blackened ashes.

Only then did the tears come. Paz wrapped Podkin in her arms, and the two of them cried for a long, long time.

———

Dawn the next morning was the start of a new day but also the start of a new life, it seemed to Podkin.

All the fighters were heading their separate ways. The forest Wardens, propping up their wounded, were the first to go. Mo Grim bowed low to Podkin and Paz.

"You will always be welcome in the Grimwode, Chosen of Hern," she said.

"Your crown," said Podkin, pulling Blodcrun out from his pack. "You should take it back."

Mo Grim shook her head. "It is yours now. Take good care of it."

She squeezed Podkin's shoulder with a grip that nearly crushed him, then turned to Chief Hennic. From a pouch at her belt, she produced an acorn, which she gave to him.

"Plant this in the ashes of the funeral pyre," she said. "It will grow into a big, strong tree. For us all to remember."

"To remember," he repeated.

The Wardens all smiled and bowed to their new friends, then turned and lumbered back to the forest. Pocka looked back over his mother's shoulder, waving tearfully to Pook, who was most upset. First his wolves had left him; now his giant best friend. Lady Enna tried to mop his eyes and stop him from crying so loudly.

Next, the bonedancers prepared to leave. Carrying something wrapped in black cloth, Zarza and her sister walked up to where the tribal chieftains stood.

"Paz and Podkin," Zarza said, bowing before them as Mo Grim had done.

"How can we ever thank you, Zarza?" Paz said. "Without you, the battle would have been lost."

Zarza shook her masked head. "I think it was you two who won the battle. Yet again. All we did was give you a little time."

"I'm sure that isn't true," said Podkin, blushing beneath his fur. "You were all amazing."

Zarza bowed her head again, then held out the wrapped

object to Podkin. He pulled back the cover to reveal an oval mirror set into a carved wooden frame.

"You asked how we knew to come," Zarza said. "This is what told us. Godseye, the mirror of Spinestone."

"Is it a Gift?" Paz asked. Podkin knew it was already —he could feel the familiar buzz of power running through it.

"It is. Sometimes it shows things that are happening in other places. We have never understood how or why it chooses to do so. It showed us the Gorm marching a few days ago, and you preparing to fight them."

"It's beautiful," said Podkin. He looked into the glass but saw only himself looking back.

"It is for you, Gift-Bearers," Zarza said. "It will be a great loss to our order, but it is clear you are meant to have it. All the Gifts seem to be making their way to you."

"Thank you," Podkin managed to say, overwhelmed. To be responsible for so many precious treasures . . .

"But we don't need it, do we?" Paz said. "The Gorm are gone now. The Balance has been restored . . ."

Zarza shrugged. "Who knows what the future will bring? And who is to question the will of the goddesses?"

Bowing again, she turned to leave. Syrena, her sister, bowed too and blew Pook a kiss, which stopped his crying, at least for a moment.

With the bonedancers marching behind them, Zarza and her sister started the long trek back to their temple.

And that meant it was time for the rabbits of Silverock and Dark Hollow to leave too.

There was much clasping of wrists and slapping of backs. Nothing brings rabbits together like fighting for their lives with one another. Even Uncle Hennic looked a little sad at saying goodbye.

He stood before Lady Enna for a few moments, both of them waiting for the right words to come. In the end, they clasped paws and nodded. Perhaps they'd never be friends, but at least they had come some way along the path.

"Goodbye, Uncle Hennic," Podkin said when his mother's awkward farewell had finished. "I expect you want your bow back now."

Hennic paused for a long time, eyes flicking to where Crom stood, holding Soulshot. It was obvious he *did* want it back, but after what Mo Grim and Zarza had both done, how could he come out and ask for it?

"Perhaps we could just look after it for a while?" Paz said, stepping up to join them. "We have eight of the other Gifts, after all . . ."

"Yes," said Hennic. "Look after it . . ."

"We'll take very good care of it," said Podkin.

"And you can have it back when we're sure we don't need it again," Paz added.

"Well," said Hennic, "I suppose . . ."

"Thank you, Uncle," said Podkin.

"Yes, thank you," said Paz, smiling. And they hurried away before he could change his mind.

———

The march back was slow and somber. Everyone seemed to be doing a lot of thinking. Podkin among them.

How much has changed in just a couple of days, he said to himself. *What do we all do now? Do we carry on living in the forest? Or do we go back to our old warrens? What happens to Crom? Or Mish and Mash? Will Yarrow want to stay?*

It was too much to think about on top of everything else. He kept looking back to where his mother walked, helping support Auntie Olwyn. It didn't look right without Brigid.

They reached Silverock, and the Dark Hollow rabbits decided to pack up their camp and head home right away. Everyone seemed eager to get back to the safety of their own beds and their own fireside.

It was as he was wrapping up his blankets that he found it. A strip of bark covered with neat Ogham writing and signed with a little picture of a sickle. He took it straight to Paz.

"It's a letter from Brigid," she said, the words catching in her throat.

"She knew she wasn't coming back from the battle," said Podkin, feeling the tears start to well in his eyes again.

"Of course she did," said Paz. She took a deep breath, then began to read:

My dear Podkin and Paz,

Please forgive me for leaving you this note. It is too hard for me to tell you this in person.

You see, I know I shall not survive the coming battle. I have known it for a long time. Don't be sad, my dears. It was meant to be, and I have had a good, long life. It has been a happy one too, especially the last months.

I have one final message for you, Podkin. One more thing you must do.

You must gather all the Twelve Gifts together. Keep them safe in the forest, where Hern himself protects you. I don't know what you will need them for, but need them you will. Other than that, I have no more prophecies left to tell you. The future is yours to work out.

I will be looking out for you both from the Land

*Beyond, Goddess willing. I knew for many years that
I was going to meet you three children. I did not know
how much I would come to love you.*

Your true friend,

Brigid

———

It was on the trip back to Dark Hollow that Podkin made up his mind.

They had set up camp halfway through the forest. Unlike the last time, Podkin knew there *were* beasts out between the trees. Saber-toothed wolves and horned giants with cloaks of cobwebs and fur. And they were all his friends.

He and Paz had taken a spot by the fire, with Pook curled up between them. Their little brother had spent the last ten minutes howling into the trees, waiting for an answer from his wolf brothers and sisters, and had tired himself out.

"What will you do now, Paz?" Podkin asked. The flames of the campfire crackled lazily, and all around them, rabbits were murmuring together softly or beginning to snore.

"Well," said Paz, "I know Mother wants to go back to

Munbury. To build the warren again. Pook will be going with her, and we should too, I think."

"But what about Brigid's message? About gathering the Gifts and keeping them safe in the forest?"

Paz flicked her ears. "Crom could do that, maybe. If he wants to, that is."

Podkin shook his head. "I've decided I'm going to stay at Dark Hollow. I will do what Brigid wanted and keep the Gifts. We have nine, so there must still be three more out there somewhere. I need to find them, to bring them together. For her. I don't think I could go back to Munbury, anyway."

He remembered the last time he had been there: that final glimpse of his father, standing across from Scramashank—holding his ground, ready to die for his tribe. He knew he would see it again every time he set foot in the longburrow. Every breakfast, lunch, and dinner. There was no way he could face it.

"But you're the next chief!" Paz said. "You have to go back!"

Podkin shook his head again. "Remember what I said in the Grimwode? You'd make a much better chief. I'm going to talk to Mother in the morning."

There wasn't much else to say after that. Both rabbits sat and watched the flames until they fell asleep, leaning against each other.

And so that was what happened.

Podkin stayed at Dark Hollow, guarding the Gifts and training to be a fighter and a leader with Crom, who decided to stay too.

In fact, quite a large number of rabbits who had escaped to the forest chose to make Dark Hollow their home. Mish, Mash, Rill, Sorrel, Tansy, and Burdock the farmer and his family. The forest warren was once again a homey and bustling place.

Lady Enna was surprisingly keen on Podkin's idea and returned to Munbury with Pook and Paz, the new chief-in-waiting. There were a few more Munbury rabbits among the refugees and survivors who went with them, and many more who had hidden in and around Munbury itself. They soon had the place repaired and looking cozy. Podkin missed them terribly, but they promised to visit regularly, and they had been gifted some of Uncle Hennic's sparrows, so they could always keep in touch.

Yarrow was the only rabbit who decided not to settle down. Much to Pook's dismay, he announced that he was off to travel the Five Realms. His ballad of Podkin One-Ear and the Gorm was almost finished, and it needed an audience.

"The world needs to know," he said to Podkin. "So it never happens again. Don't dig too deep."

"Don't dig too deep," Podkin repeated. "You will come back, though, won't you?"

"Oh, yes," said Yarrow. "I have a sneaking suspicion that little brother of yours has the bard's gift. I reckon I'll be needing him for an apprentice in a year or two."

And that was that.

Once everyone had gone their own way, the days fell into a routine of their own. Podkin woke each morning, checked the Gifts in their special chamber, then trained with Crom before sitting on the council and dealing with the running of the warren.

He ate in the longburrow each evening, slept in his room each night. Sometimes there were sparrows with notes from Paz (he had to learn to read Ogham to decipher them) or squiggles from Pook. Every other month, they came to visit him, and those were happy times.

Once or twice a week, Podkin would wander into the forest, just off the path, where the trees were thicker and the moss deeper.

He would stand silent for long minutes, staring into the shadows between the trunks. Most of the time he saw nothing, but every now and then he picked out the gleam of amber eyes or the swish of a bushy tail. Sometimes he saw the outline of a tall, horned figure. It might even seem to raise a paw to wave at him — it was hard to tell.

But he never again, not in his forest at least, saw a rabbit clad in spiked iron with eyes of blank, rusty red.

And for that, he thanked the Goddess.

Judgment

—◦∿◦—

The bard takes a deep breath and waits. He isn't expecting any applause, but not getting drop-kicked into the weasel pit would be nice.

There is a beat or two of silence, broken only by the jiggling of Rue on his seat—he is trying his hardest not to cheer, and instead is making a kind of high-pitched squealing noise, like a very plump, furry kettle on the boil —and then there *does* come some applause.

A very definite *clap, clap, clap*. It takes a moment for the bard to realize it is coming from Sythica herself. The bonedancers' eyes all swivel to the Mother Superior. Even from behind their bone masks, the bard can tell they are as shocked as he is.

"Very good," Sythica calls. "Very good. I can see why you have such a fine reputation."

"Thank you," says the bard, bowing low. He doesn't want to push his luck, but... "Um... I don't suppose this means... that you're *not* going to execute me?"

"Of course I'm not," says Sythica—this time Rue does let out a little cheer, and then quickly slaps his paw over his mouth. "Any fool can tell this is a true account of events. You were completely right to tell the story as it is. The descendants of Vetch should never have taken out a contract on you."

The bard lets out a very deep, heartfelt sigh.

"And of course, seeing as you are actually Pook Lopkinson himself, there was never any danger of our order harming a whisker on your head."

This takes the bard completely by surprise. That was *his* plot twist, his bombshell, in case of an emergency. "I... what... how did...?"

"Come now, Wulf. Or should I say, Pook? We are the bonedancers. We have our ways of finding out *everything*. You don't deny it, do you?"

For a moment, the bard *does* consider denying it. It's a secret he's grown used to keeping, and what's more, he didn't want Rue finding out this way. The little thing might actually explode. But then he is still standing on the

lip of a giant weasel's pit. A very hungry giant weasel. "No," he says. "I don't deny it. I am Pook."

For the first time in his entire tale, there is a gasp from the assembled bonedancers. A gasp and a thumping sound as little Rue falls backwards off his bench and onto the stone floor.

"I thought so," said Sythica. She makes a gesture with her hand, and all the bonedancers stand at once, bow their heads to thank him, then begin filing out of the hall. One of them pauses to pick up Rue and carry him over to the bard, setting him on his feet. The little rabbit is in such a state of shock, all he can do is stare at the bard, his mouth silently opening and closing.

"*What?*" the bard says. "If I'd known it would shut you up so well, I would have told you ages ago."

A few moments later, the hall is completely empty except for Rue, the bard, and Sythica. She gets up from her throne and walks slowly down the steps until she is standing before them.

"I *thought* it was you, but I had to be sure." She bows her head to the bard. Behind her mask, her eyes are smiling. "Please forgive the theatrics. You were never really in any danger."

"Do I know you?" the bard asks. His ears begin to tremble.

Sythica looks around the hall, making sure they are alone, then reaches up and removes her mask. It reveals an old rabbit with white fur and piercing blue eyes. And a heart-shaped patch of gray on her nose.

"Syrena!" The bard stares, speechless.

Syrena — now Sythica — smiles and reaches into a pouch at her belt. She pulls out a yellowed casting bone carved with a single rune.

"It is time I returned this to you," she says, taking the bard's hand and pressing the bone into it. "Nixha did not want me to die that day. She chose you to make sure I didn't. I owe you a debt. The bonedancers and all of the Five Realms owe you and your family a debt."

"It's so good to see you," says the bard. There are tears in his eyes. "And Zarza? Your sister?"

Sythica points to one of the banners lining the hall. The mask embroidered there has a familiar pattern on it, the bard realizes.

"She fell in battle fifteen years ago," says Sythica. "But not before *she* became Sythica herself. She was Mother Superior here for many years before Nixha called her home."

"She was a very brave rabbit," says the bard.

"She was. And she thought *very* highly of your family."

The bard smiles at Sythica. So strange meeting her

again, and after so many years. A sudden thought occurs to him.

"What will you say to the Golden Brook rabbits?" he asks. "Won't they be angry that you've refused their contract?"

"We will tell them Nixha does not wish you to die. Not at our hands, anyway. And then we will make sure they understand you have the bonedancers' protection."

"Your protection?" says the bard. "Thank you very much, but what does that mean, exactly?"

Sythica smiles, and her eyes glint an icy blue. "It means that, should they decide to hire any other assassin to take on the job we refused, the bonedancers will visit them in their warren."

"Ah," says the bard. "And that won't be a nice visit, I presume?"

Sythica's eyes glint even colder. "Let's just say none of us will be needing to kill any beetles that day."

———

Once the reunion is over, Sythica dons her mask again and escorts Rue and the bard out of the chamber. Their packs, stocked with fresh food and water, are given back to them, and they walk between two rows of bowing bonedancers all the way to the entrance (a great honor, Sythica informs them).

With more thanks and the promise that they will always be welcome at Spinestone, the doors are opened for them, and they are free to leave.

They wave goodbye and walk a little way along the road through the swamp, listening to the boom as the great doors close behind them. Once all is quiet and they are hidden from sight among the tall reeds, the bard bends over, hands on his knees, and lets out a loud, long whistle.

"By the Goddess's daisy-coated undercrackers," he says, "I didn't want to admit it, but part of me thought I was a goner."

Rue's mouth had stopped opening and closing a while back. Now his voice returns to him.

"You're Pook! You're actually, really, actually Pook!"

"I know," said the bard. "I have been all my life, in fact."

"I can't believe you didn't tell me!" Rue shouts. "That means you're the brother of Podkin! In real life! And Paz, too!"

"I am," says the bard. "How do you think I tell the story so well?"

"I thought it was the bard's magic, like you told me!" Rue stops shouting for a second as a thought hits his little head. "Hey, are Podkin and Paz still alive? Can you take me to meet them? Can you? Can you?"

The bard considers telling Rue that he has sat in the longburrow with the real Podkin almost every evening of his short life. But that would perhaps be too much for the little rabbit to take in right now.

"Of course," he says instead. "One day. We'll meet them one day."

"Why did you change your name to Wulf?" Rue asks. The first of many, many questions. "Was it because of Truefang? Or was it to keep your identity secret? Or to protect Podkin from some terrible danger?"

"Don't get carried away," says the bard. "Pook was actually just my nickname. My full name was Pookingford Lopkinson. You'd change your name if that was what your parents called you. I did love that wolf, though. It was months before I stopped howling at the moon . . ."

"I can't believe it!" Rue begins dancing along the path ahead of the bard, shouting and waving his arms. "This is the best day ever! My master is Pook! And he's not going to be eaten by a weasel! And Paz and Podkin beat the Gorm! They killed Scramashank and destroyed Gormalech! The Five Realms are saved! Gormalech is gone! Hooray!"

The bard watches him go, along the western road that leads out of the swamp, off to Thrianta and Hulstland and a whole host of new stories and adventures.

He is a free rabbit again. Free to enjoy having an apprentice, free to pass on his tales and gather new ones. Rue is happy, and life is good.

He waits until the young rabbit is safely out of earshot and then says in a low, sad voice, "Silly little rabbit. Gormalech gone? Did you really think killing a god would be that easy?"

Only the buzzing mosquitoes and rustling swamp reeds hear him. But even they seem to stop for a moment.

And shiver.

CHARACTER LIST

Thornwood Warren

THE BARD — an aging storyteller with piercing green eyes and dyed swirls in his fur. He travels the Five Realms, telling tales. Some say he is the famous bard Wulf the Wanderer. Others just keep out of his way because he is so grumpy.

HUBERT THE BROAD — chief of Thornwood Warren. A huge lop rabbit with far too many children.

RUE HUBERTSON — the seventh son of Chief Hubert. His dream is to become a bard, and he has taken the first step along the way, becoming an apprentice to the bard himself. Has more questions than there are stars in the sky.

Munbury Warren

PODKIN — son of the chief. A one-eared rabbit who became a legend. Wielder of Starclaw, the dagger, and Moonfyre, the brooch, as well as gatherer of the Twelve Gifts.

PAZ — daughter of the chief, elder sister of Podkin. Wielder of Ailfew, the magic sickle of Redwater.

POOK — son of the chief, youngest brother of Podkin and Paz. Likes soup. A lot.

LOPKIN (deceased) — chief of Munbury Warren. Wielder of Starclaw. Killed by Scramashank of the Gorm.

LADY ENNA — wife of Chief Lopkin, mother of Podkin, Paz, and Pook. Captured by the Gorm but rescued. Sister of Chief Hennic of Sparrowfast Warren.

OLWYN — Lady Enna's sister. Also captured by the Gorm and rescued.

The Gorm

SCRAMASHANK — once Chief Crama of Sandywell Warren, became possessed by Gormalech and turned into the Gorm Lord. Wielder of Copperpot, one of the Twelve Gifts, which is now warped into a horned iron helm.

MILA — once a priestess of Blackrock Warren, she was turned into a Gorm while visiting Scramashank's warren. She later stole Blixxen, the staff, Gift of Blackrock, and as a witch-rabbit, turned it to evil use.

Dark Hollow Warren

BRIGID — a witch-rabbit, daughter of the overthrown chief of Redwater Warren. She lived in the woods for years before meeting Podkin, Paz, and Pook. She uses her skills as a healer and her knowledge of the future to guide Podkin on his quest.

CROM — once heir to the chief of Dark Hollow, Crom left to lead the life of a warrior. He fought alongside Podkin's father, Lopkin, but was blinded in a battle with the Gorm and Mila the witch-rabbit. He ended up working as a sellsword in Boneroot, where Podkin, Paz, and Pook found him. He serves as their guardian and adviser.

MISH AND MASH — dwarf rabbit twins from the Eiskalt Mountains. They were traveling the Five Realms as part of a troupe of players with a sideline in attacking the Gorm. They were captured by the villains Quince and Shape and held prisoner in Boneroot Warren before being rescued by Podkin. They scout and fight, as well as train the new inhabitants of Dark Hollow.

RILL — originally from Blackrock Warren, Rill was rescued from a Gorm camp by Podkin. She is on the war council of Dark Hollow.

DODGE — a gray-furred rabbit from Muggy Pit Warren. Part of the Dark Hollow war council.

ROWAN — a sable rabbit from Ivywick Warren, also part of the war council.

SORREL — a blacksmith from Applecross Warren. He revealed the hiding place of Surestrike the hammer to Podkin and later forged the Gormkiller arrows with it.

TANSY — another lop rabbit from Applecross. She joined the quest for Surestrike but had to turn back after being injured. She assists Sorrel in the forge.

YARROW — a wandering bard who joined Dark Hollow as part of his mission to write an epic saga about the Gorm. He later became Pook's master and eventually the High Bard himself.

VETCH — a ginger-furred rabbit from Golden Brook Warren. Briefly part of the quest for Surestrike, he then worked in the kitchens of Dark Hollow, which is where you end up if you annoy Crom too much.

FARMER BURDOCK — rescued from the Gorm by Podkin and his group, Burdock, his wife, Dandelion, and their children live in Dark Hollow.

Hern's Holt

MO GRIM — chief of the Wardens of Hern's Holt. She leads the Wardens and cares for all the elements of Grimheart Forest.

VENDRA — plant Warden. Cloak of vines and leaves, horns of woven roots.

BOLE — tree Warden. Cloak of leaves, horns of tree branches.

CHITNA — insect Warden. Cloak of living beetles, horns of giant stag beetle. Mother of Pocka.

POCKA — still a baby, Pocka will one day be Warden of mushrooms and toadstools.

RAKE — animal Warden. Cloak of wolfskin, horns of antlers.

VIAN — bird Warden. Cloak of feathers, sparrow-hawk wings instead of horns.

COB — spider Warden. Cloak of cobwebs, horns carved like spider legs.

LITHERUS — reptile Warden. Cloak of shed snakeskin, horns carved like striking vipers.

TRUEFANG — gray-furred, saber-toothed giant wolf. Alpha of the first pack to join Podkin against the Gorm. Pook wanted to keep him as a pet.

DEADEYE — black-furred, one-eyed, saber-toothed wolf. Alpha of the second Grimwode pack.

NIGHTCLAW — brown-furred, saber-toothed wolf. Alpha of the third Grimwode pack.

Spinestone

ZARZA — bonedancer: a follower of Nixha, the goddess of death. A novice when Podkin first met her, she took part in the quest for Surestrike.

255

SYRENA — Zarza's sister. An initiate of the bonedancer order, she had yet to carve her bone mask.

SYTHICA — the Mother Superior of the bonedancers. The finest, most experienced warrior is chosen to become Sythica when the current one retires.

Other Rabbits

UTHRIC (deceased) — once chief of Sparrowfast Warren. Father of Enna, Hennic, and Olwyn.

HENNIC — chief of Sparrowfast Warren. Brother to Enna and Olwyn, uncle to Podkin. Current owner of Soulshot, the bow, one of the Twelve Gifts. Not the nicest of rabbits.

AGBERT — chief of Silverock Warren, husband of Agwen. Very fond of bees.

THE
TWELVE
GIFTS
OF THE
GODDESS

—∾—

STARCLAW - Munbury Warren

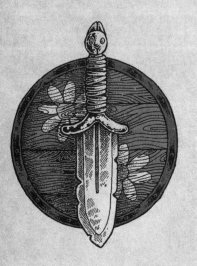

A copper dagger that can cut through anything (except iron).

CURRENT OWNER:
Podkin

AILFEW - Redwater Warren

A small sickle that glows to show poison (its real power of controlling plants is unlocked when the Balance changes).

CURRENT OWNER:
Paz

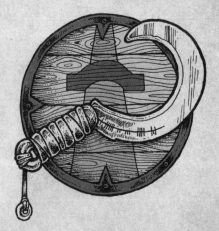

MOONFYRE - DARK HOLLOW WARREN

A silver brooch that lets the wearer jump between moon shadows.

CURRENT OWNER:
Podkin

SURESTRIKE - APPLECROSS WARREN

A smith's hammer that can forge Gorm-piercing weapons.

CURRENT OWNER:
Podkin

DEATHWAIL - Crowskin Tribes

A singing spear that returns to the thrower.

CURRENT OWNER:
Graven, Crowskin chief

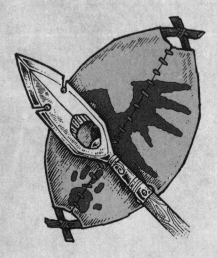

BLIXXEN - Blackrock Warren

A staff that can call down lightning.

CURRENT OWNER:
Podkin

STORMCLEAVE - Am Ul Warren

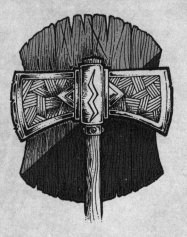

Two-handed battle axe that blasts out thunder.

CURRENT OWNER:
Unga, chief of the giant rabbits of Am Ul

BLODCRUN - Hern's Holt

A horned crown that lets the wearer read minds.

CURRENT OWNER:
Podkin

MAGMAROK – Temple of Fyr

An anvil that heats any metal placed on it, without a forge.

CURRENT OWNER:
High Priest of Fyr

COPPERPOT – Sandywell Warren

A helmet that makes the wearer invulnerable.

CURRENT OWNER:
Podkin

SOULSHOT - SPARROWFAST WARREN

A bow that never misses its target.

CURRENT OWNER:
Podkin

GODSEYE - SPINESTONE

A mirror that lets the viewer see what's happening in different places.

CURRENT OWNER:
Sythica, Mother Superior of the bonedancers